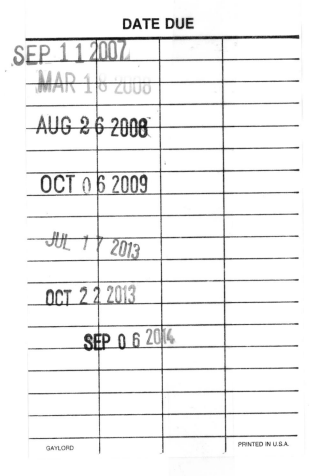

DATE DUE

SEP 11 2007		
MAR 18 2008		
AUG 2 6 2008		
OCT 0 6 2009		
JUL 1 7 2013		
OCT 2 2 2013		
SEP 0 6 2014		
GAYLORD		PRINTED IN U.S.A.

SOCCER CHICK RULES

Also by Dawn FitzGerald
Getting in the Game

Dawn FitzGerald

SOCCER CHICK RULES

A Deborah Brodie Book Roaring Brook Press NEW MILFORD, CONNECTICUT

TO SOCCER CHICKS EVERYWHERE.

Thank you to my first readers and family—John, Ryan, and Brynn. In appreciation for my parents, Tony and Gaye, and siblings— Tami, Sean, Tara, and Dana. For former teammates and coaches at Clarkstown High School North, New City, New York, and the University of Rochester—good times on and off the field! Thank you to Deborah Brodie, who has the heart of an athlete and the eagle eyes of a great editor. A special thank-you to the Girls' Varsity Soccer team at Orange High School, Pepper Pike, Ohio—I'm so happy to be your Coach Fitz—*Now, take a lap!*

A Deborah Brodie Book
Published by Roaring Brook Press
Roaring Brook Press is a division of Holtzbrinck Publishing Holdings
Limited Partnership
143 West Street, New Milford, Connecticut 06776

Library of Congress Cataloging-in-Publication Data

FitzGerald, Dawn.
Soccer chick rules / Dawn FitzGerald.—1st ed.
p. cm.
"A Deborah Brodie Book."
Summary: While trying to focus on a winning soccer season, thirteen-year-old
Tess becomes involved in local politics when she learns that all sports programs
at her school will be stopped unless a tax levy is passed.
ISBN-13: 978-1-59643-137-9
ISBN-10:   1-59643-137-7
[1. Politics, Practical—Fiction. 2. Soccer—Fiction. 3. Schools—Fiction.
4. Taxation—Fiction. 5. Family life—Ohio—Fiction. 6. Ohio—Fiction.] I. Title.
PZ7.F572Soc 2006
[Fic]—dc22
2005027062

10 9 8 7 6 5 4 3 2 1

Book design by Patti Ratchford
Printed in the United States of America
First edition September 2006

CHAPTER ONE

"Open in the middle!" I shout across the field to my teammate Katie. Without even glancing up, she sends a sweet lofting pass that lands just outside the penalty box. I fight past the defender to get at the ball and give it a hard kick toward the yellow net in front of me.

Cling! It strikes the metal crossbar on the goal and ricochets back in front of the goalie's outstretched arms—just out of reach. Now it's a matter of who wants it bad enough as the offense and defense battle for the ball.

I hear the sound of shin guards smashing together and I feel a sharp jab in my back. My friend Brittany, who's playing fullback for the red team, practically growls in frustration, fighting to get her foot on the ball and to prevent my team— green pinnies—from scoring a goal. After all, the stakes are high. Coach always makes the losing team sprint extra laps at the end of practice.

The black-and-white Brine ball pops loose, and I barely get my left foot on it. The kick is weak and the goalie scoops it up in her arms with a relieved smile on her face. She cradles it for a moment, catching her breath before she has to punt it downfield.

I stand next to her, panting from exhaustion and disappointment. Glaring at the ball, I'm tempted to kick it out of her arms and commit a blatant foul, but Coach blows the whistle and shouts, "That's it for today, girls! Tie score—everyone runs extra laps!"

"*Nooo*, Coach!" Both teams groan as we take off our sweaty pinnies and head toward the bench for a quick gulp of water before the run.

"And, Tess Munro, work on that left foot!" Coach shouts.

"I know! It's just that I couldn't—"

"No excuses!" she says with a faint smile on her face. "You make excuses in practice and you'll wind up making them in a game and then it'll carry over into your schoolwork and—"

"Okay, Coach, I get it!" I say as I begin to run the figure eight, jogging the end lines and sprinting the sidelines of the field. But somehow, I can't see my science teacher, Mr. Metzer, accepting "I couldn't get a foot on it" for a late lab assignment.

⚽

"The universe is expanding like a huge, colossal fart stinking up the room," says Mr. Metzer.

Has Metz completely flipped out? And does he expect us to write this stuff down?

Everyone laughs.

To prove Metzer's point, Bo Tauber lets one rip, which sets off a chain reaction of copycat farting among the boys. It sounds like we're in the trumpet section of the middle school band instead of science lab.

Olivia Fletcher glares at Bo and says, "Pig!"

He gives her a friendly snort and carries on.

I *almost* tell her not to worry. With two older brothers, I'm practically an expert on farts. Bo's was loud and forceful. It's the silent ones, originating from deep bowel space, or as Metzer would say, "black holes," that are the most deadly.

I say nothing to stuck-up Olivia. Instead, I doodle my name and a picture of a soccer ball with my green gel pen—Tess Munro, Tess Munro, Tess Munro. I've got the name down. It's the soccer ball that needs work. It looks like a bunch of raisins on a plate.

Olivia kicks Bo's chair with her leather boots in a lame effort to make him stop.

My best friend, Ibby Bloom, has one hand cupped over her mouth and nose while the other waves in the air to attract Metzer's attention.

"Question, Ibby?"

"Will this be on the test?"

Leave it to Ibby, science geekess and germ-a-phobe, to worry about Metz hitting us with a pop quiz. Aren't there more important things to worry about? Like whether the stupid school levy passes next month and we have sports for the rest of the year? Hello—Earth to Ibby! Where are your priorities?

She's on the school swim team, but probably because it's the only sport where chlorinated water immediately washes away sweat. For Ibby the formula is simple: *Sweat + bacteria = germs.* I totally blame her mother for this. When we were little, she carried around a quart-sized bottle of disinfectant gel whenever we went out in public.

"Isabelle," she'd say, "clean your hands." Ibby would hold them up like an offering and would promptly receive two quick pumps of purification. In addition, Mrs. Bloom trained her daughter to avoid doorknobs, hand railings, elevator buttons, and escalator grips. For Ibby, simply using public bathrooms and water fountains requires tricky maneuvers involving elbows, feet, and wads of tissues.

"Ibby," Mr. Metzer says, hands clasped behind his back as he rocks from heel to toe, "*everything* discussed in this class is fair game on a pop quiz or test. Now, let's get back to our gaseous galaxy!"

This inspires the boys to release yet another round, which Metz wisely chooses to ignore. Zipping my hoodie up until it covers my mouth and nose, I roll my eyes at Bo through the narrow peephole. You gotta love the kid, best goalie in the soccer league, but sometimes he carries things too far. Ibby's got the right idea after all, and fleece offers excellent filtration.

⚽

My parents would kill me for admitting this, but basically sports are the only reason I bother to attend school. Everything else is just warm-up or pregame—nine classes and lunch before the main event. Ever since I was in kindergarten, the highest grade on my report card is always for gym, or Phys Ed as they call it at Clarkstown Middle School. "Gym is the name of the room," says our Phys Ed teacher, Mr. Wadler.

I argue with my parents that surely that lone A+ balances out my crappy performance in other subjects. They don't buy it. Besides, you don't stand a chance of winning an argument when your mother's a trial lawyer and your father's a school psychologist.

I'm not a dumb jock, though. It's just that nothing, *n-o-t-h-i-n-g*, I ever learned in school comes close to having as much meaning for me as athletic competition. I love how powerful I feel when I'm playing a game—any game. Just so long as it involves teams, a ball, hoops, a bat, or a goal. Throw in some cool uniforms and I'm so *there*!

Sports have purpose and meaning. Pre-Algebra, the Napoleonic period, iambic pentameter? *Please*—I'd gladly ditch it all. My only concern is that the voters in our small Ohio town find it in their hearts and wallets to vote "Yes!" for the school levy on November 2.

Which explains why I'm giving up precious practice time on the soccer field this afternoon to attend a student levy meeting after school. Normally, I never get involved in politics. I'm not the girl who walks around wearing slogan T-shirts or a collection of multicolored rubber wristbands for every imaginable cause. And you definitely won't see my name on the Student Council roster, running for class office, or heading up the magazine drive.

But when the school district put the athletic programs on the line—foul move, by the way—I figured a jockette's got to stand up for something other than a pop fly. Besides, athletics aren't the only thing that will go if the vote is no. There'll be no more busing or after-school activities, and some of the newer teachers will lose their jobs.

I can always walk to school or risk my life hitching a ride with my high school brother, Mark, who failed his driver's test three times (speeding through a school zone, hitting a parked car while attempting to parallel park, and running over the neighbor's garbage cans—with his front tires) before finally getting his temps this summer. Big deal if a few teachers are fired and the classrooms are overcrowded. But I promise this—I won't go to school if there's no soccer, basketball, and fast-pitch softball to get me through the state-mandated 180 days. *No way!*

❂

A new math teacher, Ms. Harper, stands in front of a flip chart, writing down a list of activities we're brainstorming for the levy campaign. Her anxious smile adds a personal dimension to those job cuts if we fail.

"Only four weeks until the vote!" cries Olivia Fletcher for the third time during the meeting-that-never-ends.

I give Bo a look—*We gave up practice for this?* He reads my mind and, ever so carefully, picks up the eraser from the chalk tray. Hopefully, to nail Olivia in the head with it if she opens her big mouth one more time.

If I had known that Olivia would be in charge of this committee, I'd have ditched the idea of getting involved. Yet, before I can sneak out the door to practice, I'm signed up to help with yard signs, a Halloween haunted house fund-raiser, and door-to-door canvassing of my neighborhood. What the heck is *canvassing* anyway?

Why would Olivia take charge? She's a cheerleader, not an athlete. Although my mom says that for Title IX law—gender equality—schools actually count cheerleading as a sport. Gimme a break! I guess if we lose sports, Olivia loses her excuse for parading around school on Spirit Days in plastic-wrapped tops and skirts that barely cover her butt. It's not like she can just pick up and cheer for the chess team: *Checkmate! Check-queen! We really rock this scene!*

Maybe the cheerleaders have something at stake after all.

Ms. Harper explains, "Your interaction with the public, especially the elderly, who almost always turn out in large numbers to vote, could make a big difference in how they vote. Please remember in the upcoming weeks to be positive, helpful members of our community."

Bo leans over and whispers, "Does this mean no more practicing slide tackles on little old ladies in the park?"

I smile. "Yeah, right." Bo's grandmother practically raised him and he treats her like she's the queen of England. "Who are you kidding, Tauber? Everyone knows you're a sucker for old ladies with walkers."

"Four! More! Weeks!" squeals Olivia, clapping her hands together for emphasis like she's on the sidelines cheering for a football game.

Bo's goalie arm instinctively whips forward, propelling the eraser across the classroom until it smashes against the far wall, exploding in a mushroom cloud of chalk dust inches above Olivia's head. "Yikes!" Olivia ducks.

We make a run for the door, but Ms. Harper follows us into the hallway. "Bo Tauber, that's *exactly* the kind of behavior I'm talking about!"

Bo shrugs and jogs backward for a few steps, giving Ms. Harper one of his trademark sorry-I-didn't-mean-it looks. With his sense of humor, mischievous grin, and springy caramel-colored dreadlocks spiraling out of his head, most teachers find him hard to resist.

"Don't tell me you didn't mean to throw it!" she scolds.

Bo laughs. He knows she's going to let him off. "Actually, Ms. Harper, I didn't mean to miss!"

⚽

I hate to miss. As a forward, I know it's my job to score the goals for the team, and somehow, I usually find a way to make it happen—head balls, volley kicks, or just plain muscling it in between the goalposts. Coach says that I have a sixth sense for scoring. My mom says she can always tell when a goal's about to happen by the determined look in my eyes and how my ponytail whips back and forth as I fight my way through the defense.

"You're late!" Coach shouts when she sees me jogging toward the field. "Run four laps, then stretch it out."

"Sorry—went to a levy meeting after school."

Eyebrows raised. "Levy meeting, huh? Now, detention I can see. . . ." She looks at me with a twinkle in her eye and gives her whistle a shrill blast. From the side of her mouth, she says, "Levy meeting—that's a new one, Munro."

"I'm serious, Coach. I want to help. I'll die if they cut sports!"

She laughs, "Me too, or at least have trouble paying my bills."

I jog along the white-lined perimeter of the field. Pushing myself to run harder with each lap, I feel my lungs bursting with

☉ CHAPTER TWO

When I arrive home after soccer practice, Dad's sitting in the easy chair with his reading glasses balanced on the tip of his nose. There's a pile of school folders in his lap and even more scattered all over the floor. Names are written in black permanent marker on these folders—troubled students—who need to see the school psychologist for one reason or another. Dad's great with other people's kids' problems, but I wonder how he'd react if Luke, Mark, or Tess Munro's folder ever landed on his lap?

"How's practice?" he asks.

"Pretty good, except that I was late because of a levy meeting. Coach made me run extra laps."

"Oh?" he murmurs, absorbed in his work. "Sounds reasonable."

"Yeah, well, I hope people in this town are *reasonable*."

Dad nods.

Wonder what the folder says—drugs, multiple personalities, chronic truancy? "It's not fair," I say. "Last summer, they cut the Cleveland Rockers, our first professional women's basketball team. The U.S. Women's Soccer League bit the dust. And our professional women's football team, the Cleveland Fusion—bet you their days are numbered!"

Dad responds with an enthusiastic, "Hmm!"

I try his favorite subject—psychology. "I'm developing

the crisp October air. The trees surrounding the field look like they're on fire—blazing orange, red, and gold leaves. Overhead, a noisy flock of Canada geese fly by in a graceful moving V.

Soccer season is my favorite. We begin in late August in the heavy heat of summer, and by the end of the season, we might be kicking the ball around in the snow. Extremes—that's the way I like it. Which explains why, even though I'm not crazy about taking orders from Queen Olivia, I plan on giving 110 percent to this levy campaign. If I treat it like it's a game, then how can we possibly lose?

attachment issues. I'll never learn to trust if every team I root for disappears. *Poof!* Gone!"

More paper shuffling from the Buddha-belly in the reclining chair.

Time to bring out the big guns. "Dad, if they cut school sports, it'll totally *suck!*"

Bingo!

He hates it when I use "unladylike" language, even though *suck* is pretty tame in Tess Munro–land. From tagging along after my older brothers and their friends, before I even entered preschool, I was basically tutored in just about every foul word. They made up a Curse Word Alphabet and they'd quiz me: "Hey, Tess, what's the *A* word? *B, C, D* . . . ?"

To them, nothing was funnier than a smut-mouthed baby sister in diapers. I clean up my act, though, around my parents. And Dad's tuned in enough to realize that I'm really upset, because he doesn't warn, *"Language,* young lady!" Instead, he gets right to the heart of the matter. "It's business, Tess, pure and simple."

I drop my two-ton backpack on the floor. It lands with a loud crash. "Then I'm making it *my* business!"

Chuckling, he finally puts aside his papers and reaches out for a hug. "I know you will!"

After dinner, I head outside with a clipboard and sign-up sheets. According to Ms. Harper, canvassing a neighborhood means that you knock on front doors and ask people to agree to allow their names to be listed in the local paper, endorsing the levy. Then you ask them to display a pro-levy yard sign on their front lawn a couple of weeks before the election.

No problema!

I know most of our neighbors and have trick-or-treated at every house in this neighborhood since I was a little kid. How hard can it be? But when I step outside, the first house I face across the street is the O'Hanlons'.

The O'Hanlons moved in last June. The three girls in the family all attend St. Jude's Parochial School. St. Jude—the patron saint of lost causes. *Not* a good sign. How will I convince them to support the public schools and poke a levy sign in their perfectly manicured front lawn?

Besides, we don't actually get along.

This past summer, my brothers swear it was Mrs. O'Hanlon who called the city on us because our front lawn was a little overgrown. Okay—I admit, it was a freaking forest. If a Frisbee or baseball happened to land in it, we'd just shrug and go into the garage and find a new one. Mr. Metzer would categorize our lawn as the black hole of Bluebird Drive—objects fall in, never to be seen again.

Basically, it was a power struggle over mowing the grass. Dr. Dad, with all his psych training, insisted on leaving it up to the three of us to take responsibility and work out a schedule. His motto—communicate and *cooperate!*

Luke, Mark, and I ignored the two Cs. "Hey," my brothers would reason, whenever I suggested we tackle the growing problem, "we're showing Mom and Dad school spirit by letting these dandelions reach the three-foot mark. It's a tribute to the official flower of the University of Rochester—their alma mater."

"Oh yeah?" I said. "Their school mascot's a yellowjacket. You guys prepared to take a stinger in the butt for school spirit, too?"

They called me a smart *A* and told me to shut the *H* up.

By mid-July, a city official came and cited us for breaking some lawn-care law. I guess one person's flower is another person's weed. Not only was our yard an eyesore, it was also a pollen and ragweed hazard for allergy sufferers in the neighborhood.

Mrs. O'Hanlon crowed with victory from her front yard the day she spied us weed-whacking and then finally mowing our way through the jungle. At that time, I remember wondering why Mark collected and saved all the dandelions that had gone to fuzzy seed. Later that night, I watched from my bedroom window as my brother sat on the sidewalk in front of our house, blowing wishes and sending silky dandelion seeds swirling across the street.

At the meeting today, Ms. Harper had stressed, "Every vote counts!"

No matter how much I'd like to, I can't skip the O'Hanlons' house. Taking a deep breath, I feel my stomach flip-flop as I cross the street and walk up the front steps to ring their doorbell. It's not the turf war that has me worried, or the fact that a ton of dandelions has recently invaded their front lawn. My biggest worry is Jillian O'Hanlon.

Jillian's in the ninth grade and makes Olivia Fletcher look like best-friend material. Believe me, I tried to make friends with Jillian. One day, Bo and I saw her outside, showing her younger sisters how to do perfect cartwheels and backflips.

It was at the end of summer, when you're getting a little bored of the whole vacation thing, and Ibby was still away at camp. Bo and I were hanging out on my front steps ping-ponging the phrase "I don't know, what do you want to do?" back and forth, until we noticed the gymnastics exhibition going on across the street and decided to check it out. After hellos, I asked Jillian, "Want to go to the park and kick a soccer ball around?"

"Hmm." She wrinkled her turned-up nose, and brushed long dark hair from her tan face. "I don't *do* soccer." But then her pale eyes focused on Bo, and she suddenly changed her mind. "Maybe for a little while, though."

Bo makes everyone change their mind.

"What sport *do* you do?" Bo asked as he tossed the soccer ball from one hand to the other.

"Dance," she said, spinning with a flourish. She turned and walked away to tell her mom where she was going. On the back of her short shorts, right across her butt, were the sparkly letters *D-a-n-c-e*.

I pointed and asked, "Does she need a reminder?"

Bo shoved me and laughed, but I could see Jillian's *Dance* had Bo's total attention—or maybe he's a slow reader.

On our way to the fields by the park, Jillian had a million questions—all for Bo. "Where do you live? Do you play for Clarkstown High School? No? I can't believe you're only going into the eighth grade—you're *sooo* tall!"

Gag me.

By the time we made it to the field, Bo's ego was as inflated as my brother's blowfish in our aquarium. I considered it my duty as a good friend to knock the air out of him.

When he stepped between the goalposts—still totally into Jillian—I lined up the ball for a direct kick at the beautiful dreads that he's been growing since third grade.

Thwak!

My laces connected with the soccer ball, sending it flying through the air toward my intended target. My aim may have been a little off, though. Soccer Chick Rule Number 1 - Never Kick a ball in anger.

Next thing I know, Bo is rolling on the ground, clutching—well, you get the picture. In a game situation, he would have had his fullbacks lined up in a defensive wall in front of the goal. He also would've been wearing a cup for protection and definitely wouldn't have been flirting with some bimbo on the goal line.

Jillian cried, "Oh my God—are you okay, Bo?"

Duh? The boy got nailed in the nuts. Nurse Jillian obviously didn't grow up with brothers.

Curled in a fetal position with his hands between his legs, Bo groaned pitifully.

Kneeling down beside him, Jillian asked, "Should I call 911?"

I rolled my eyes. What next? Mouth-to-mouth resuscitation?

In apparent agony, Bo twists his face into the ground and swears. Sounds like, "*F*-word *b*-word, Tess!" Although, I could be wrong. It's hard to understand someone with grass in his mouth.

I wanted to say "I'm sorry." Should've warned him that I was taking the shot. But instead, I stood there mute, clenching and unclenching my fists.

Jillian glared at me. "What did you do that for?"

"You don't know soccer," I said.

"I know an *idiot* when I see one!"

It was at this point in our budding friendship that I thought, (a) we've got nothing in common, and (b) I hate her guts!

Whispering something to Bo, she stood up in a huff, brushing dirt off her hands, and then, thankfully, danced her little butt home.

My face felt like it was on fire.

I called after her, "Oh yeah? Well, only an idiot would have *Dance* on her shorts!"

Really lame, Tess.

"Bo?"

No answer.

Guilty, I walked over and sat down beside him. Elbows leaning on the weapon of mass destruction—the soccer ball— in my lap, I said, "Hey, Bo?"

Groan.

Gently, I poked him in his back. "Sorry. I wasn't aiming. If you want, I'll run home and get a bag of frozen veggies. Ice always helps."

His shoulders shook a little.

"You should've paid attention. We came up here to play soccer and all you were doing—"

Muffled laughter.

"Hey, what the—?" I grabbed his arm and tried pulling him around to see his face. "You're faking!"

Deep belly laughs. He looked up at me, grinning, tears of triumph streaming down his face.

I punched his arm. "Faker! I knew I didn't hit you that hard! Now she thinks *I'm* the jerk!"

Bo grabbed the soccer ball and stood up. "Come on. Got rid of her, didn't I?" He extended his hand and pulled me up. "Now, let's practice. Forget Jillian."

But I can't. Standing here at her front door, the whole scene comes rushing back to me. School started soon after that, and I had no contact with her. If I get up the nerve to ring this doorbell, what are the chances that the O'Hanlons will agree to support the public-school levy?

Maybe no one's home or they're not finished with dinner yet. They could be doing homework and it wouldn't be right to interrupt. *Every vote counts!* I kick the concrete step, picturing Ms. Harper's earnest face. Teachers have no idea of the power they have over us.

The poodles start barking before my finger even touches the glowing doorbell, which gives off a buzzer sound—game over. Gotta go!

Commotion and footsteps, as someone fiddles with the lock. I chant under my breath, "Anyone but Jillian, anyone but Jillian, anyone but—"

"Jillian? Umm . . . hi!"

Cold stare.

Actually, *stare* is way too neutral a word to describe the look Jillian O'Hanlon gives me. Suddenly, I have a surge of compassion for the Jehovah's Witnesses and the CUTCO knife salespeople who knock on our door regularly.

"I—I'm collecting signatures." I wave my levy clipboard in front of her face, ignoring the involuntary flinch. Did she think I was going to hit her with it? Hmm, props are powerful. Props make me feel official, legitimate, and businesslike. *It's business, Tess.* Right!

From behind the screen door, Jillian perfects her you-are-lower-than-a-slimy-slug stare.

I do my talking-slug impersonation, my words sticking and stumbling off my lips. "Would your parents sign this . . . uhm . . . endorsement and maybe . . . put up a yard sign for the school levy?"

"I don't know," she says.

Our mutual dislike for each other filters through the screen door.

"Could you please go ask them?"

"No."

"Why not?"

"Because."

"Because why?"

"Not home."

I smack the clipboard against my hip and run my hand through my long brown ponytail. *Ding-ding!* First round goes to Jillian. But I'm not giving up. "I'll come back later, then."

She opens the door and sticks half her body outside. She's

wearing those spongy toe dividers between freshly painted purple toenails. "Don't bother," she says. "My parents wouldn't
vote for your stupid levy, anyway."

"Why not?" I tick the points off on my fingers: "You use
our buses, our fields, and our auditorium for graduation. If the
levy fails, we lose busing, some teachers, all sports—"

"I've seen how *you* play sports, and I think it'd be a good
thing to get a beast like yourself off the field."

I sense that Jillian doesn't mean this as a compliment.

I step closer, and she quickly ducks back inside. *Click*—and
locks the screen door.

"What are you talking about? You've never seen one of my
soccer, basketball, or softball games. You don't know how I
play."

"I've seen you practically kill someone—for fun!"

"You mean Bo?" I press my face closer to the screen and
lower my voice. "He totally played you. Faked the whole thing
that day up at the field."

"I know what I saw. Now, get off my property!"

The poodles bark and growl like pit bulls, scratching their
painted nails on the screen. "It's not *your* property," I remind
her, "and I'll be back to talk to your parents." I wave the clipboard in front of her face, again.

She doesn't flinch this time, but instead slams the door in
my face.

I march down the steps and across the front lawn. Wow,
there really are a ton of dandelions! It looks like an organic
herb farm, except that the O'Hanlons spent the big bucks and
hired a chemical company to come out and poison their lawn,

posting little warning flags—*Keep off! Hazardous to children, pets, and pregnant women.* Too bad earthworms and birds can't read.

On the sidewalk in front of Jillian's house, I write on my clipboard next to the name O'Hanlon, *Maybe? Check back later.*

Soccer Chick Rule Number 2 - Even when the odds are against you, it never hurts to think positive.

CHAPTER THREE

Monday morning, wearing latex gloves and holding a Popsicle stick, Nurse Bicknell takes the annual back-to-school lice check seriously. What's crazy is that they expect us to carry on with class, ignoring Bicknell as she lumbers from student to student, picking through our hair like a silverback gorilla preening the troop.

What if she finds a crawling critter or an egg or two? What is she going to do? Pull the fire alarm? Embarrass the kid by awarding an early dismissal pass and a parting gift of insecticide shampoo?

It's humiliating. But I guess compared to the annual spine check for scoliosis—where Bicknell makes you bend over in your bra and panties in her office while she judges your potential as the next Hunchback of Notre Dame, a few pokes in my hair is nothing.

I try to concentrate on Ms. Poe's history lesson. She had us read an essay by some guy named Swift—*A Modest Proposal*—but neglected to tell us that Mr. Swift was only kidding when he suggested that the British eat Irish children for dinner. He even offered a few recipes. Colleen Fitzpatrick went to her guidance counselor, crying hysterically. I hate it when teachers get us all worked up for nothing.

Bicknell's just about to impale Ibby's curly red hair with her Popsicle stick when Ibby says, "Please stop!"

Surprised, Bicknell utters a few sharp words, which Ibby ignores, covering her head and shaking it *no*.

I can guess what this is all about. I give Bo a knowing look, but he's too busy adjusting his seat for a better view.

"Isabelle, is there a problem?" asks Ms. Poe.

"I don't want to be rude, but Mrs. Bicknell uses the same gloves and stick on everybody."

Nurse Bicknell's jaw drops and she holds her latex-encased hands in the air as if they were freshly scrubbed for surgery. Her voice shakes. "I'll have you know, you impertinent girl, that I've been a school nurse for over thirty-five years and never—*never*—have I had any trouble during the annual lice check. This is for your safety, mandated by the Ohio State Board of Health, and you have no right to refuse!"

Poor Ibby. I totally see her side. When we were in first grade, everyone couldn't wait until it was their birthday because we got to wear this special hat for the entire school day. Unfortunately, when it was Ibby's turn, that hat gave her lice. It took Ibs's freaked-out mom multiple washings with smelly tar shampoo and hours of combing every night to pick the nits out of Ibs's thick, curly hair. Her mom threatened to have Ibby's hair cut off.

But that wasn't the worse part. When Ibby returned to school after the treatments, some mean kids on the playground ran around tagging each other and saying, "Ibby Bloom bugs—you're it!"

If Nurse Bicknell thinks she can win this one, she's underestimating her opponent. Ibby may be small, but she's determined and smart. Which is why it doesn't surprise me when she quietly gets up from her desk and stands, arms crossed, in front of Ms. Poe's current-events bulletin board, titled FIGHTING OPPRESSION AT HOME AND AROUND THE WORLD.

Bo chants, "Bug-free, Ib-by."

"Remember when she had lice in first grade?" Olivia whispers. "I think you can be a carrier."

"Shut up, Olivia," I say. "We *all* had lice in first grade." Geez, go to school with the same kids for ten years and you've got no privacy.

"That's enough!" says Ms. Poe. "Isabelle, will you agree to the check if Mrs. Bicknell changes her gloves and uses a new stick?"

"Yes."

Bicknell's eyebrows meet in a straight line across her forehead. With a displeased grunt, she throws the old stick in the garbage and peels the rubber gloves off her sweaty hands—*snap-snap!*

She takes an especially long time checking Ibby's hair, and once, Ibby cries, "Ouch!"

Ms. Poe turns from the chalkboard. "Are you finished yet, Mrs. Bicknell? *My* curriculum is also state-mandated, and frankly, you're disrupting the learning process."

Yay, Ms. Poe!

I'm next. And even though I know Ibby's hair is so clean that I could use it as dental floss, I remind Bicknell to use a new Popsicle stick for me as well. Soccer Chick Rule Number 3 – Always support your teammates!

☻

Speaking of nit-picking, Olivia Fletcher is driving me crazy. Every day she grills me about my levy assignments: "How many people have you signed up for yard signs? Do you have the endorsements for the newspapers? Where are you holding the haunted house fund-raiser?"

She never lets up until she's sucked all the air out of a room, leaving the rest of us suffocating in her presence.

I actually do have some good ideas for the haunted house. In fact, the solution to the location is so obvious that I can't believe that I hadn't thought of it before. There's just one problem. A big one—getting Ibby's mother to say yes.

"Come on, Ibs!" I bring the topic up during lunch. "You know your home's the perfect place for the haunted house. It's practically a castle." Ibby's father, professor of Medieval English at Oberlin College, has a passion for architecture. He designed their home to look like a castle, complete with turrets, winding staircases, and even a small mote—minus piranhas and crocodiles, of course.

"Are you crazy, Tess? You know what my mom's like. How do you think she'd handle a bunch of middle school kids running through her house, dripping fake blood? Oh my God—the dirt! She'd totally freak. She'd be ready for an insane asylum before the night was over."

"We need people dressed up to scare the customers. Crazy people in straightjackets, foaming at the mouth—your mom would be great!"

"You're the one who's lost her mind. There's no way. *No way* my mom will ever agree to it."

"Ibs, remember when we were in third grade and you

wanted to go to Jeremy Finkelstein's party at the Burger Barn? You thought your mom would never let you eat E. coli patties or play on those germy toys. But she surprised you and let you go!"

"Oh, I remember. She packed sterile gloves and a surgical mask. She gave me alcohol wipes to sanitize the tables before we ate!"

I crush my paper lunch bag into a tight ball. "Okay, so it would freak her out if she actually *knew* about it. Didn't you tell me she's traveling a lot lately for that company she works for? What if she's out of town the weekend we have the haunted house? We'll have it all cleaned up before she gets home, and she'll never know anyone was there."

"Tess," she grabs my shoulders, "my mother knows if one of her perfume bottles is moved a fraction of an inch on her dresser. She knows if I snuck a soda pop, because of the extra can in the recycling bin. You really think we could have a house full of"—she looks around the cafeteria—"middle schoolers gone wild, hyped up on caffeine and candy, rampaging through her home on Halloween, and after it's all over, *she'd never know anyone was there?*"

"Maybe?"

Ibby jams a spoonful of organic yogurt into her mouth. "The trouble with you is that you won't take no for an answer."

"The trouble with *you* is you won't take a chance! At least ask your dad. I bet he'd go for it. He'd think it's a great idea. He loves showing people your home."

Ibby sighs—wavering, wavering. "No!"

"Tell you what," I say, eyeing the garbage barrel positioned at the door about thirty feet from our table. Gripping my paper bag ball in my hand, I line up the shot. "I make this basket and you have to at least *ask* your parents."

"*Nooo.*"

"Come on. Half the battle is believing that something can happen—even when the odds are against it." I squint at the garbage can.

She smiles reluctantly and makes an attempt to snatch the ball from my hand and block my shot.

"If I sink it, you ask if we can use your home for the haunted house. I miss and it's all over. Case closed! We'll have to use the dusty old American Legion Hall or the smelly school gym. Deal?"

She studies the distance from the wastebasket to our table and finally agrees, "Deal!"

"Here goes." I run through my basketball preshot routine, remembering Coach's acronym—BEEF: *B*alance. *E*lbows in. *E*yes on basket. *F*ollow through. I launch the paper ball off the tips of my fingers, and it sails over six tables, past two lunch monitors, just misses pegging Ryan Burke in the nose, and lands in the center of the garbage pail.

"*Yes!*" I pump my fist in the air.

"That'll be a detention for you, little Miss Sure Shot!" shouts the lunch monitor as she whips out her referral slip to write me up.

Ibby shakes her head, looking apologetic. "Dumb bet, Tess. Now you've got detention."

"Don't feel bad, Ibs. It's not the first, and besides, it'll be worth it if your parents say yes."

✪ CHAPTER FOUR

Before I even set foot on the field, Coach shouts, "Late again, Munro. Five laps, then stretch it out!"

"Sorry, Coach."

"What was it this time? Jazz band? Power of the Pen? Unity and Diversity club?"

"No . . . detention."

"What?" The whistle drops from her mouth. "Can't hear you." She cups her hand to her ear.

"Detention."

"Detention? Now, that I believe. What'd they nail you for this time?"

"Throwing a paper ball from thirty feet away at the garbage pail during lunch."

"Thirty feet—you make it?"

"Yep."

She laughs. "Now, get running!"

It helps when your soccer coach also coaches girls' basketball.

I have plenty of time to think as I run my laps. Like how much I love basketball and wouldn't want to see it cut this winter if the levy fails, and how I don't have one single name down on my list yet for yard signs. I had better kick up the canvassing after dinner tonight. At this rate, there'll be only one sign displayed in the neighborhood—on my own front lawn.

Practice is amazing this afternoon. The late afternoon sun

feels warm, but a cool breeze keeps us comfortable throughout the drills. The forwards work on shooting and it feels good to see most of my shots sail past the goalie's outstretched arms and into the back of the net. On the field next to ours, where the eighth-grade boys' team is practicing, Bo is doing a great job in goal—only he's blocking most everything that comes his way.

The best part of practice, though, is at the end, when coach blows her whistle and shouts, "Bring it on in for a scrimmage!"

Today, she surprises us when she announces that we're going to scrimmage the boys. I high-five my teammates and we shout, *"Yesss!"*

It doesn't matter if it's a spelling bee, a review game in Social Studies, or battle ball in Phys Ed, whenever a teacher or coach says "Boys against the girls," we're psyched! Boys absolutely hate to lose to a girl. That makes us try even harder to beat them.

Bo, tossing a soccer ball and wearing a confident smile on his face, walks over to our field with his teammates and calls, "Hey, Munro! We're going to shut you down today. You're not coming anywhere near my goal!"

"Your goal? *Hello?* Last I checked, this was the girls' field, and those are *our* goals, so why don't you get in there, Tauber, so I can drill it past your face?"

He shoves me playfully. "Don't trip!"

"Hey, Coach!" I call. "Yellow card for the goalie who can't keep his big mouth shut"—I push him back even harder—"or his paws to himself!"

"Knock it off, you two," she says as she assigns positions.

We take the field, waiting for Bo's coach, who volunteered to referee, to blow the whistle for the start of the scrimmage.

Girls have the kick-off, and Alison and I set up about five yards from each other on the midfield line so she can give me the short forward pass to begin the game. When I feel the ball at my cleats, I give a quick shoulder fake and dribble around John King as I look to send the ball to the wing.

With a lofting pass, I send Alison flying on the wing. But the halfback, Alex Wooley, a stocky, aggressive player, won't let Alison dribble around him so easily. He kicks the ball out of bounds on the sidelines for a girl's throw-in.

Our halfback throws the ball in to Brittany, who cuts and turns, creating an open run down the wing with Alex chasing at her heels. She sees me wide open in the middle and crosses the ball to the top of the penalty line.

Bo charges out of the box to try to intercept the ball and cut my angle for the shot.

Chest trap, thigh, volley kick off my right cleat—*bam!* The ball rockets into the upper left corner of the net just as Bo dives, a fraction of a second too late for the save.

Girls' goal—one to nothing!

No jokes or smiles from Bo as he gets up off the ground and kicks the grass with his cleat.

"Offsides!" shouts Alex.

"Was not!"

"Goal's good," says the boys' coach. "Quit doggin' it, Wooley, and you won't get burned next time."

Which is the problem. The boys want to win as badly as we do. They just don't want to look like they're trying too hard to do it.

Bo's team scores soon after that, and the coaches let us

battle hard for another twenty minutes or so as the sun sets behind the fields. It's getting late and there's a caravan of cars lined up in front of the school—parents waiting to pick up their kids after practice.

When the final whistle blows, ending the scrimmage, we're tired, thirsty, and tied at 1–1. Jogging in to get a drink from our water bottles and gather up our stuff, Bo says, "To be continued, Munro."

"Lucky for you!" I tease. "Another minute and we would have put one in the net—right over your head."

Bo tosses the ball at *my* head, but I duck out of the way, forcing him to run and shag it in order to put it into Coach's mesh ball bag.

"Ever heard of a head ball?" Bo says as he jogs past me, tapping me on the forehead with his gloved hand.

"Can't afford to lose brain cells—Geometry test tomorrow."

"Since when are you worried about brain cells or Geometry?" he calls over his shoulder.

"Since getting a D on the last quiz."

Bo walks back with the ball tucked under his arm. "Keep that up and it won't matter if the levy passes. Your crappy grades will keep you from playing sports."

"Thanks, Mr. Brainiac. Why don't I move 'study more' to the top of my to-do list?"

⚽

By the time I finish dinner, studying for Geometry has sunk to the bottom of the list, again. Mom's working late preparing a brief, and Dad gives me the green light for a little door-to-door action after I help clean up the kitchen with Mark.

"You want dishes or sweeping the floor?" Mark asks.

"Floor."

"Nope, you had that last night. You got dishes."

"Mark, I want to go outside before it gets too dark," I plead.

"Then rinse 'em and load 'em fast, girl."

I fling the A-word at him. He counters with a few choice words of his own and a taunting smack across the face for good measure. Head down, I try for a quick punch–kick combo, only to find myself in a headlock, with Mark's laughter in my ears.

"Daaad!" I call. You'd think I'd have figured out the routine after living with my brother for thirteen years now. He enjoys a good fight, and now that Luke's off at college, he feels like the supreme sibling of the house. Even though our shouts are getting louder and louder, Dad won't rush to my rescue. "Let the kids work it out for themselves" is his philosophy.

Unfortunately, "no blood, no foul" is Mark's.

Twisting and kicking, I try to land one. "Let go! Or I'll tell Dad that you were fooling with those CDs in the car the other day and that's how you hit the curb and lost the hubcap!"

Mark may be ruthless, but he's reasonable. Releasing me, he says, "Okay, okay—here's the deal. I sacrifice and do the dishes and sweep the floor tonight because I'm a great guy and I want you to get those yard signs up."

Safely out of range, I give him an obscene hand signal depicting my idea of up.

Outside, the crickets chirp their prefrost songs and the Elliotts' Border collie, Laddie, barks at a squirrel teasing him from the top of the fence. Across the street, the Gordons' house is decked out for Halloween.

Mom told me that when she was a kid, Halloween decorations consisted of a carved pumpkin lit with a candle on front-porch steps. That's it. Today, houses have ghostly strobe lights; full-size caskets with fake headstones on the front lawn; and motion-activated, life-size witches, goblins, and ghosts that screech at trick-or-treaters.

Nothing's simple anymore. You've gotta go over the top in everything. Which is why the fact that I've failed to sign up a single house for a yard sign is beyond pitiful.

It's not that I'm discouraged or afraid to knock on anyone's door after that scene with Jillian O'Hanlon and her attack poodles. It's just that I can barely find the time to complete all the things I need to do in a normal day—school, soccer, homework. Add yard signs, and it's no wonder everything, including my grades, is slipping lately.

The other night, I heard Dad counseling a parent over the phone, "Children are too hurried these days. We need to slow it down for them. Carve out time for them to be kids and help them enjoy childhood." While he spoke, he was rushing around the house gathering his papers, eating dinner standing up, and putting on his coat and shoes to leave for a school board meeting that had started over fifteen minutes ago.

Soccer Chick Rule Number 4 – Never rush your shot.

I will not rush. I'll take my time and patiently knock on every door and sign people up, one by one. Besides, I'm sure to have better luck in the evening now that most people are home from work.

At the end of my driveway, I hesitate. Lights are on across the street at the O'Hanlons', but I think I'll skip that scene tonight. I turn right on the sidewalk and figure I'll try the Workmens. Although they're elderly and don't have any children in the school district, they're always friendly and never complain about the variety of balls—tennis, golf, football, soccer, and kickball—that have landed in their backyard over the years.

I knock on the door. Mrs. Workmen has a goofy pumpkin wreath hanging up and I can see the living room light on behind it.

Knock again.

No answer.

I give the doorbell a ring, and a minute later, Mrs. Workmen invites me in. I remember all the warnings that teachers have given us since kindergarten, about always using the buddy system and never going into someone's home when you're selling something door-to-door—because let's face it, I'm selling something. And if I don't find any buyers soon, I can just kiss school sports good-bye.

Inside, I'm struck by the fact that everyone's home has a unique smell. Bo's smells like the dried flowers his grandmother has arranged in bouquets and wreaths all around the house. Ibby's is a cross between lemon furniture polish and new car smell, and Mrs. Workmen's smells like homemade cookies and medicine.

She explains, in the kindest manner possible, that they are on a fixed income, and with the rising cost of medical care for Mr. Workmen's emphysema and her diabetes, they may not be able to afford the projected monthly increase of a new levy. "But we have grandchildren of our own, sweetie, and we'll try to find a way to make it work."

Mr. Workmen's oxygen tank and bed are set up in the living room, and I realize that from the picture window, he has a clear view of our front lawn and all of the O'Hanlons' across the street. Did he see me knock on Jillian's front door?

"In my day, we played Kick-the-Can, Spud, or hopscotch in the streets. Didn't need uniforms and organized school sports to have fun," says Mrs. Workmen. Then, she explained in great detail the strategy and rules of Spud.

I can just picture it—an interscholastic Spud team or competing for medals on the All-County Kick-the-Can squad. What would the medals look like? Crushed soda-pop cans hanging from yarn necklaces?

What can I say? "But I want to play soccer, basketball, and fast-pitch softball—with cool uniforms!" sounds like I'm totally missing the point.

Mrs. Workmen sends me on my way with some fresh-baked oatmeal cookies. They're warm, old-fashioned-tasting, and real. Not the prepackaged-cookie-dough kind that we make at home.

I apologize to them for even asking for their support. "Don't worry, Mrs. Workmen," I lie. "Spud sounds like fun."

Outside, under the streetlight, the words on the clipboard blur as I write next to the Workmen name, *Probably no, but they'll think about it.*

Note to self: Never go into sales. You couldn't sell a steak bone to a starving dog.

CHAPTER FIVE

Bing, bong, binnng! The chimes, indicating that morning announcements are about to begin, sound a little off-key today. Every two weeks, they rotate the student announcers chosen from Mr. Ramella's Drama class. You'd think Drama would be an easy A, but Ramella's a hard grader, and so far, unbelievably, the only person I know who's gotten an A this year is Bo. Apparently, he wowed Ramella with his impression of a dying Orc from *Lord of the Rings* and was rewarded with a two-week stint as student announcer.

Ramella's making a huge mistake. A dying Orc is one thing. Bo Tauber armed with a microphone in front of a captive audience—that's just asking for trouble.

"Wake up out there, bed-heads!" shouts the familiar voice over the PA system. Everyone in my homeroom laughs, and most recognize Bo's voice. "Hey, it's Taub! Taubman. Yay, Bo boy!"

"Quiet during announcements!" hisses Mrs. Uridel.

"Urinal," someone snickers from the back of the room.

"*Shhh!*" she insists, finger up to her mouth in a classic librarian pose, which is surprising since she teaches Spanish.

"Hellooo, Clarkstown cool cats! This is Bo-the-beast Tauber, coming at you from the main office, where the secretaries are hot and the coffee's cold—"

Abrupt loud crackling sounds are heard over the PA, and then silence.

Homeroom boys pound the desks, laughing. Uridel's shushing us so hard she sounds like a deflating bus tire.

"That was the shortest announcing debut in the history of the school," says Ibby.

"He'll be back," I predict.

Sure enough, we hear a loud click. "I'm *baaack!* Sorry, we're experiencing a little technical difficulty here in office-land. Moving right along and comin' at ya with today's announcements!"

Bo reads them out loud, managing to mangle not only the room numbers for the after-school meetings, but also the dates and times. I guess he forgot to mention to Ramella that he's mildly dyslexic. We overhear Mrs. Korn, the vice principal, in the background, correcting Bo item by item.

In closing, the announcer is supposed to lead the school in the Pledge of Allegiance. Only, when Bo comes to the part where he's supposed to say, "And to the Republic for which it stands . . . ," he substitutes his own version. "And to my soccer team for which I stand, one goalie, between the posts, blocking shots and penalty kicks from all!"

Static again—silence.

No chimes signaling the end of announcements. Boy soccer players in our homeroom go wild, chanting, "Bo, Bo, Bo!" The bell rings, dismissing us from homeroom.

It rained earlier this morning, and in the hallways, we hear the *squeak-squeak-squeak* sound of our sneakers against the tile floor. Ibby and I take a quick peek in the girls' bathroom mirror on our way to Metzer's for Science.

"Why does it always have to rain on picture day?" asks Ibby.

"Look at my hair! It's so frizzy, you'd never know that I spent over an hour blowing it dry this morning."

"Forget your hair. Look at my humongous zit! Whenever anyone looks at our eighth-grade yearbook, they'll see Tess Munro with Mt. Vesuvius on her chin."

"Don't make eye contact with it," advises Ibby. "If you stare at it, it'll just grow bigger. Here, dab a little Purell on it."

"Isn't that for cleaning your hands?"

"Yes, but it's sixty-two percent rubbing alcohol. Maybe it'll dry it up before pictures this afternoon."

I laugh and dab. "Come on, Ibs. Metz hates it when we're late."

The bell rings as we walk in the door. Metz looks up from his laptop computer. "Third tardy, Tess. You'll need to serve a detention."

I wonder if he'd let me off if I told him I was in the bathroom formulating a scientific hypothesis on pimple eruptions.

"From the earliest moments of the history of the universe," says Metz, "protons smashed into each other, producing radiation. This accident, at the beginning of time, resulted in extra particle matter. Look around you—we're here today because of a series of cosmic accidents. We're here because stars explode. All of you are made up of the same stuff as stars!"

Wow! Impressive . . . I think. But I can't concentrate because I'm too busy running my finger over the ginormous bump on my chin, imagining that it's about to have a cosmic accident of its own.

Georgie Taxus's hand shoots up in the air. Last month, his

mother petitioned the school board to put warning stickers on all Science textbooks: EVOLUTION IS JUST ANOTHER THEORY!

Georgie pesters Metz like an annoying horsefly whenever the topic of evolution comes up in class. We should have warned Metz. Georgie can't help it. Last spring, his father sold a bag of potatoes on e-Bay, claiming they resembled Jesus and the twelve apostles—"spiritual spuds" he called them. High bid was $79.99 for the bunch.

The rest of the day goes downhill from there. Some jerk pulls the fire alarm and we have to stand outside for twenty minutes in the rain until the fire department gives the all-clear. Mrs. Korn comes over the PA and says that they're in the process of studying the video from the hallway surveillance cameras to determine who the prankster is and, rest assured, he or she will be prosecuted.

By picture-taking time, Ibby's hair has expanded like a Chia Pet on steroids and my zit looks like a third eye. Thank God, I have soccer practice today after that stupid levy meeting. Kicking the ball into the back of the net is the only thing that will make this day worthwhile.

How come bared teeth is a sign of aggression in the animal world, but in humans is supposed to mean friendliness? Olivia's false smile doesn't fool me one bit.

"I understand, Tess, that you're busy with soccer, school, and whatever," she whines, "but you and Bo are in charge of the haunted house and yard signs, and so far, you're totally letting us down!"

"I don't mean to," I say. "I just haven't . . ." Oh, why am I wasting my time at this meeting when I could be outside, like Bo, who's ditched this to go to soccer this afternoon. "I'm working on it, Olivia. I just don't have any definite answers yet from the people I've contacted."

The problem with canvassing my neighborhood is that I take too much time at each house. After being at the Work-mens' for half an hour and at the Henrys' for another twenty minutes or so, while eighteen-year-old Amanda Henry quizzed me on Luke's love life at college, there just wasn't time to knock on any more doors before I had to get home and study. And I'm still waiting to hear what Ibby's parents say about the haunted house. "Some things take time," I tell her.

"But, there's only three more—" Olivia catches herself, eyes darting around the room, ready to duck incoming objects. A look of relief on her face—Bo's absent.

Instead, I promise to get back to them tomorrow on the haunted house and double my efforts with the yard signs by spending all day Saturday and Sunday knocking on doors, until my knuckles bleed. That ought to make Olivia happy. She understands blood sports, at least when it comes to cheering from the sidelines.

⚽

When I finally make it to soccer practice, the only thing that changes is the number of laps coach makes me run as punish-ment for being late again.

"Six today, Munro."

As I complete my last lap, Coach shouts, "Next fall, you ought to go out for cross-country with all the long-distance mileage you're racking up!"

"Ha!" I say, sprinting to her side. Putting my arms over my head, I struggle to catch my breath. "How would you win any soccer games, then?"

"Humble little smart-aleck aren't you!" she teases. "I lose you anyway, toots—remember, you're up at the high school next year. And I can guarantee you, Coach Magaletta is not going to put up with tardies to practice."

"It's for a good cause," I say as I finish stretching.

"I know, Tess, and you're a good kid for trying. You know the rules, though. You're late. You run."

"Yeah, yeah, the rules," I mumble. I jog to the end of the line for a three-person weave down the field. With so much pent-up energy and frustration from the day, it feels fantastic to nail the ball, one-timing it into the back of the net—score!

"Nice shot, Tess!" Katie calls.

"Thanks!"

We divide our team in half and scrimmage ourselves this afternoon, and before the end of practice, I could kick myself for rushing and not putting on my shin guards for protection. Brittany, who's playing defense for the red-shirt team, nails me hard in the shin during a scramble in front of the net. Now, I have a throbbing red bruise the size of an orange on my left leg. Coach makes me ice it after practice.

On our team, soccer bruises are a badge of honor. We compare size, shape, and color—the reddish purple ones are the newest, and as the weeks pass, they turn from blue to green and finally to a faded light brown. This lump on my leg is a pulsing red mass. Alison jokes, "Hey, hematoma, what's growing on your leg?"

"Forget her leg," says Katie. "Check out the chin!"

"Shut up." I pitch a piece of ice at Katie from the plastic bag.

"Ouch!" It nails her in the back, and she uncaps her water bottle and dumps some in my direction.

"Disgusting, backwash—thanks, Katie!"

"Don't tell Ibby. She'll avoid you—contaminated!"

"It's not Ibby. It's her mother who'd want me sterilized."

"Find out about the haunted house, yet?"

"Nope. Ibs says she'll have an answer for me tomorrow."

"It'd be so cool if we could have it there. I've never even been inside Ibby's house."

"And you never will—dressed like that."

Katie basically wears the field. Sweaty streaks of dirt down the side of her face. Mud covering her entire left side, from shoulder to shorts, due to an amazing goal-saving slide tackle at the end of the scrimmage. Cleats caked with tufts of grass and dirt. Not to mention the occasional green smudges from the goose crap covering the field.

Katie grins. "Beautiful, huh?" She extends her hand. "At least we clean up well."

"Sure, potential runway models," I say, getting up off the ground. "Oowah, my shin."

"You mean, *run-away* models, which is what I'd do if I had to wear a pouty look on my face and four-inch heels on my feet! I'll take muddy cleats any day." She kicks them off and claps them together in order to dislodge the dirt and matted grass from the rubber spikes.

Slipping into our flip-flops, we follow the rest of our team to the locker room.

I take a deep breath, inhaling the smell of wet fall leaves. "This is the best time of day," I say.

The rain clouds have cleared and the western sky is a pinkish purple color, casting a warm glow all around us. It feels like the earth's being wrapped in a velvet blanket. Mourning doves coo goodnight, and in the distance, someone's hungry dog barks for dinner.

"Any time we finish playing hard is the best time of day," Katie says. She shakes the last bit of water from her bottle, sprinkling it over our heads like a blessing.

⚽ CHAPTER SIX

"I know you're in there. Wake up!" I shout as I pound on the front door with my fists.

It's 9:00 Saturday morning and I'm knocking on doors as promised. But at this particular house, it's not to sell someone on sticking a yard sign in their front lawn. It's to wake Bo Tauber up so he can help. His mom works and his grandmother volunteers on Saturday mornings, so if I can't get Bo to answer the door, I'm stuck canvassing on my own—again.

"Bo, you promised!" He probably stayed up late last night playing poker or video games with his soccer buddies, and now he figures that pounding noise is just a part of his dream, or nightmare.

I walk around to the back of the house. I know exactly which window is his. Snapping off a long branch from the overgrown forsythia bush underneath it, I tap against the screen and shout, "Bo, you're not ditching me. Wake up!"

Two little neighbor kids in protective bubble helmets are riding their bicycles up and down the short driveway next to Bo's house. They stop and stare at the crazy girl scratching on windows with twigs. I try to ignore them.

"Bo's sleeping," they call over to me.

I wave and mumble, "Not for long." Why is it that when we were little kids, we used to get up at daybreak, and now that we're teenagers, some of us can hardly drag our butts out of bed before noon? If had my own cell phone, like half the kids at school, then I could call Bo and wake him. But, "No," my mother says, "an eighth grader doesn't need a cell phone."

I need one now.

"He's asleep!" they shout. The shorter of the two gets off her pink bicycle and stamps her blinking light-up sneakers on the ground in frustration at my stubborn stupidity.

"Listen," I walk over. "I need your help getting Bo out of bed for a really important job. Could one of you go inside your house and call his phone number, and the other go to his front door and ring the doorbell, while I stay here and shout by the window?"

They stare at me wide-eyed, probably thinking that if this is what teenagers do for fun on a Saturday morning, they'll opt for the perpetual primary-school plan.

"If we all work together, we can wake him!" I try to sound enthusiastic, hoping they'll think it's a game.

"He'll get mad," says the one with the loose chin strap and runny nose.

"No, he won't," I lie. "He'll think it's a great joke."

You can't fool little kids these days. They're a suspicious bunch. When I was little, my brothers told me that I was adopted; that a killer possum lived underneath our wooden deck; and that if I drank milk through a straw stuck up my nose, it would taste like a vanilla shake. I believed every word, totally blinded by devotion and envy.

"Okay." I hit 'em with the truth—sort of. "You're right, maybe Bo won't like our wake-up call, but he promised this morning he'd help with something really important. He'd want to keep his promise—right? It wouldn't be *fair* if he didn't."

Now, I'm talking their language. *Fair* is a concept that rules their world. Especially since "It's not fair!" is the rallying cry in any home with more than one child. Which explains Bo's sometime lack of understanding in this area, as an only child.

The plan works, and within ten minutes, Bo's slamming his front door, still dressed in his pajama bottoms and T-shirt, as he ties a red bandana around his mane of wild hair.

"Are you crazy, Tess!" he grumpily complains and curses while rubbing the sleep from his eyes. "Why couldn't you sign people up yourself? You know Saturday's my only day to sleep in. My grandmother will have me up tomorrow by seven to get ready for church!"

"Sorry." I try to hide my smile behind the clipboard.

The bobble-headed bikers stare at us as we walk in front of their driveway. Bo playfully raps the tops of their bike helmets with his knuckles and teases, "I'll get you two later."

They point their fingers at me. "She made us!"

I make a face. "Thanks a lot."

"Yeah, I know. I'll take care of her, too. How about a little seven a.m. wake-up call tomorrow, Tess? Better yet, why don't you come to church with Gram and me? Two and a half hours in the morning, then back again that afternoon for a potluck dinner and more preaching, praying, and singing."

I hand him the empty clipboard. Not one single person signed up.

He looks at it and whistles. "On second thought, maybe we better skip church on Sunday. Gram always says the Lord helps those who help themselves, and if we don't get some advertising up for this levy, we don't have a prayer of playing sports next season."

⚽

By Monday morning, I'm so psyched, I practically dance through the school hallways! Bo and I signed up close to forty houses over the weekend to display levy signs. We made a game of it. He took the odd side of the street and I took the even. Because I looked at it as a race, it kept me moving along so I didn't waste time chatting with the neighbors when I should be focusing on the goal—signing people up.

There was only one thing that ruined the weekend. Sunday afternoon, when we were almost finished and heading to my house for a snack, we see Jillian O'Hanlon outside. This time, she's not cartwheeling across her front lawn half-naked or walking her yappy poodles. This time, she's talking to a tall boy with sandy blond hair wearing a faded blue Abercrombie and Fitch T-shirt. I recognize the shirt immediately because I told him he was crazy for spending so much money on one shirt. But, of course, Mark never listens to me.

"What's he doing?" I asked Bo.

"Staring at her chest?"

"Stop!" I punched his arm. "Why would he be talking to her after I told him she slammed the door in my face?"

"Slipped his mind?"

"What mind?" I mumbled as I made my way toward them.

I overheard my brother saying, "Yeah, so just tell your

parents that I'd be happy to mow their lawn, and in the winter, I'll even shovel your walk and driveway. I'm trying to save money for college."

Has the world gone insane? Mark Munro in the lawn care/snow removal business? The O'Hanlons would have to be blind to hire him. Besides, I thought he wanted to save money to buy his own car. I heard him complaining the other night at dinner after Dad banned him from driving the car for a few days because Mark smashed the mailbox at the end of our driveway and tried to hide it in the bushes on the side of the house.

Jillian smiled. "I'll let my parents know. Thanks a lot, Mark, for helping catch Maribelle." She holds the dog up in front of her and makes kiss-kiss sounds near the poodle's mouth.

Gross!

The dog remembers me and begins to squirm and growl in her arms. At least the pooch hasn't had his brains sucked out his ears, like my brother and Jillian. But I figured I better take advantage of the moment and press my case. I looked her straight in the eye. "Have you had a chance to ask your parents about that yard sign, yet?"

Jillian looked past me and said, "Hey, Bo," giving him a little wave with her painted nails.

"Hi, Jillian." Bo flashed his perfect smile.

I had a strong urge to whack him in the head with the clipboard, but then that would totally justify Jillian's opinion of me.

She struggled with the killer poodle in her arms and gave me a canine smile and said, "Oops, forgot to tell them that you stopped by. Why don't you check back sometime this week? They're usually home evenings."

Later, as Bo and I were walking into my house, he said, "Maybe she's not so bad after all."

"Sure," I said, "and maybe that was her evil twin the other day and the day before that, but today the *nice* Jillian is allowed out for some fresh air. Yeah, maybe!"

⚽

Fingers flying over the keyboard in Discovery Tech, I'm thinking about all the yard signs and hoping that Ibby will have good news for me today on the haunted house. I'm in the zone, so I practically jump out of my seat when Mrs. Bustamonte says, "I've had enough of this, class. This has got to stop!"

We stop typing.

"What's her problem?" Bo asks.

I shrug.

"Who? Who?" She looks and sounds like a tiny screech owl. "Who keeps stealing the mouse balls?" she demands.

"Not again," everyone groans.

We definitely have a mouse problem at Clarkstown Middle School.

Mrs. Bustamonte isn't upset over furry mouse balls. It's the missing gray rubber ones that have her in an uproar. Apparently, kids pry them out of the computer mouse and steal them just for kicks. Later, they reappear, rolling around the school hallways, flying over our heads on the bus, or bouncing off the walls in Phys Ed.

"If you act like kleptomaniacs, you leave me no option but to treat you as such! From now on, at the end of every class, I'll check everyone's balls to make sure they're in place."

Bo glances at me—eyebrows shooting off the top of his forehead. But Mrs. Bustamonte is very old and very upset, so he wisely keeps his mouth shut.

"Five minutes before the bell rings, you'll turn over your mouse." She sniffs. "If it's missing, you will pay to replace it, face possible suspension for theft of school property, *and* I'll send a note home to your parents!"

"Hey, yo," Bo leans over and whispers in a Mafia voice, "messa with Bustamonte's balls and she busta you face!"

I try to suppress my laughter, but it's no use. Mrs. B. is totally oblivious to a cardinal rule for teaching middle schoolers: *Never* say the word *balls* in class and expect us not to crack up.

"You find this amusing, Miss Munro?"

"No." I glare at Bo, who wears an angelic expression and says, "Give her a detention, Mrs. B. Send her to the office!"

She ignores him. "Ninety-nine cents a ball," she says, looking down her nose at me through her tortoiseshell glasses. "Add it up, and over the course of a year, your parents—hardworking taxpayers—are underwriting this senseless theft. I—I will not tolerate it anymore."

Suddenly, I feel sorry for her. My mom says Mrs. B. taught her Typing Skills class when she attended this very same middle school over thirty years ago.

Mrs. B. takes off her glasses and cleans them on her wool skirt. She sighs and says, "There will be a period of amnesty, of course. If you know of anyone who has missing balls in their locker, or you see any rolling around the school, please return them to my mailbox in the office. No questions asked."

We stifle our laughter and solemnly go back to work. That is, until five minutes later, when Bo holds up a mouse with its cord detached from the computer and says, "Hey, Mrs. B., someone castrated my mouse."

⚽

"Tess! She said yes!" I hear Ibby calling from down the hall on my way to Language Arts.

"Your mom said yes? We can have the haunted house at your place? I can't believe it!"

Ibby nods her head, breathless and laughing. "Why? You're the one who told me to try!"

"Yeah, but I didn't think that they'd actually say yes! Does she know real live people will be coming through your house—wearing shoes?"

"It was perfect timing, Tess. My dad's been after my mom for being so strict and fussy. He's encouraging her to lighten up a bit. This is the perfect opportunity—the perfect test."

"Awesome!"

"She's even agreed to help decorate and dress up for the event. She's written about twenty lists already—everything from decorations to levy slogans and theme music."

I hug Ibby. "We're going to have the *best* haunted house this school has ever seen! Wait until Olivia Fletcher hears this!"

"Girls, get to class," warns the hall monitor.

We make it in the door just as the bell rings, but not in

time to avoid Mr. Chen's reproachful look as he reminds us, "In your seats by the bell, ladies, and honor the brief time we have together."

Mr. Chen's big into honoring things. Whenever we begin a new novel, he presents it likes it's a holy gift or something. I swear he gets half the kids—who would normally cheat by reading Cliff's Notes or going online for summaries—to actually read the book just because they wonder what Chen is making such a big deal about.

Ibby passes me a note.

I try to open it underneath the desk so Chen won't get upset that I'm not paying attention to the discussion of *To Kill a Mockingbird*. But even if he did catch me, I'm confident that I'd be able to answer any questions on the book. I found it in Luke's room last summer and read it on my own. I told my mom that if I ever practiced law like she does, I'd like to be a lawyer like Atticus Finch.

Ibby folded her note into an origami flower and wrote *Tess Munro* in different-color gel pens on all the petals. It takes me a minute or two to open it.

Hey Tesser!
So psyched about the haunted house!!! Let's make plans. Mom wants me to be a medieval princess for Halloween. Nooo way! I wanna be Raggedy Ann. You be Andy?
Luv ya lots — Ibs

I write back:

Ibs—

Nice flower, girl! I'm psyched too!!! Can't meet after school. Have another Olivia torture meeting! Tomorrow away soccer game against Ramapo. We'll kick their butts!! Go Lions! Wanna sleep over Friday?

Lions Rule!!

Tess #12

P.S. Gonna be a ghost — <u>Boooo</u> Radley!

I reshape the note into a football and punt it across my desk with my finger. It goes wide and hits Olivia Fletcher on the arm and lands on the floor between her desk and Ibby's.

"Hey!" she says.

I frantically signal Ibby.

"Is there a problem, ladies?" asks Mr. Chen, who stops reading out loud an excerpt from the novel—one of my favorite parts when Scout and Jem find the carved soap figurines in the knot hole in the tree.

Before Ibby can pick up the note, it disappears underneath Olivia's Birkenstock shoe. She slowly slides it underneath her desk.

"There was a bug crawling across the floor," says Olivia.

Mr. Chen goes back to reading out loud and Olivia makes a face at Ibby and whispers, "Ibby Bloom bug."

"Give it back," whispers Ibby.

Ignoring her, Olivia pretends to follow along with Mr. Chen in her book.

I've got to get that note back before Olivia reads it! It's one thing to be a total pain in the butt; it's another to actually see it written in print. What if she shows Ms. Harper the note and they kick me off the levy committee? And after all the work Bo and I did this weekend and finally getting Ibby's parents to say yes to the haunted house!

I can't take my eyes off the corner of the note sticking out from underneath Olivia's suede shoes. Leaning as far over the front of my desk as I dare, I whisper to the back of Olivia's streaked blond hair, "Give it back!"

Ever so slightly, she shakes her head, no.

It's my own fault for mispunting. That's my problem—everything's a game. Until, suddenly it's not.

One more try. "Pass it to Ibby, then, *please.*"

Swish-swoosh goes the hair—*no!*

This calls for desperate measures. A definite plan of attack. A slide tackle?

Mr. Chen's back is to us as he writes on the board a list of all the things Scout and Jem discover in the tree over the course of the novel.

I raise my hand and contribute, "An old broken pocket watch."

"Good, Tess." The minute he turns to write on the board, I lunge out of my seat, kicking Olivia's shoe with my foot and snatching the exposed note—score! I would have made it back to my seat, too, if Olivia hadn't pushed me in frustration at having been outmaneuvered.

"Young ladies!" says Mr. Chen in a shocked voice.

Definitely not honoring our time together.

"She attacked my foot, Mr. Chen—on purpose!" Olivia cries.

"Tess?"

I clench the note in my hand and frantically try to come up with a plausible excuse. "I . . . leg cramp?" And I rub my shin for effect.

Ibby to the rescue. "It's my fault!"

I give her a desperate what-did-you-do-that-for look?

She continues, "Mr. Chen, I was so excited because my parents agreed to host the haunted house for the levy fund-raiser, so I wrote Tess a note and she wrote back and when she tried to pass it to me—well, actually, she punted it and missed and it hit Olivia by accident and Olivia stepped on the note and refused to—"

"Please!" Mr. Chen's hands are in the air. "Who has the note now?"

"I do."

"Please bring it up here, Tess."

My face feels like it's on fire as I walk up to the front of the classroom and place the note on Mr. Chen's Bob Dylan calendar. Returning to my seat, I figure that I've probably earned detentions for the rest of the week.

He picks up my tightly folded paper. "Football?" asks Mr. Chen with a twinkle in his eye.

I stare at my desk, feeling ashamed for having disrupted his lesson, but not for having kicked Olivia's shoe. I wish I'd missed and nailed her in the shin. I wait for the punishment.

"Human beings can't resist communication," Mr. Chen says, holding the note in his hand. "Sometimes the urge to reach out to one another is so powerful that we're willing to take risks."

I look up.

Ibby turns around and gives me an encouraging smile.

"Boo Radley takes a chance when he reaches out to Scout and Jem. He tries to communicate with them through the various objects he hides in the tree, and in spite of his isolation and loneliness, he takes a chance on friendship, understanding, and hope."

With a sigh of relief, I take out another piece of paper. I don't fold it into a flower or a football. This time, I'll use it to take notes instead of writing one. As I listen and write, I offer a silent thank-you to Mr. Chen, Harper Lee, and my brave friend, Isabelle Bloom. I'm not exactly sure what happened here just now, but it feels a lot like forgiveness.

And besides, teachers are always telling us that we have to learn to write the important stuff down.

"The Ramapo Warriors are going down!" shouts Katie.

I love home soccer games because we get to wear our orange Puma jerseys and have home-field advantage. But away games are fun, too, because we wear our black jerseys and get to ride the bus. On the bus, we go crazy singing songs, eating junk food, and listening to music. Coach reminds us, "Stay in your seats and keep it down back there!"

But we're too pumped for the game, and pretty soon, the noise level is right back up there again. The bus driver, Miss Joanie, is pretty cool, though. She knows we're excited about the game, and as long as we're quiet whenever she has to drive across railroad tracks and we share our soccer-ball cupcakes with her, she's happy to drive us to our away games.

In the backseat, Katie braids my hair and asks, "Did you notice that your name wasn't painted on the sports spirit window? What's up with that?"

Before games, the cheerleaders show school spirit and paint the sports teams and the athletes' names on the windows across from the office. It used to be that just the football players got a "Go Lions Football!" but now all the teams, even cross-country, are recognized.

"Yeah, I noticed. I sort of got into a fight with Olivia during Language Arts yesterday."

Katie laughs. "So she left your name off on purpose?"

I shrug. "Maybe. Are you almost done?" I reach up to touch the braids, but Katie slaps my hand away.

"Stop, you'll ruin it."

"Are we almost there?" I ask. "And what's Ramapo's record, anyway?"

"I think they're undefeated, also. Should be a good game today."

We make a sharp turn into the Ramapo Middle School's parking lot and all our junk goes flying off the seats and across the bus. We scramble to gather it all up and throw it back into our gym bags. Then we sing at the top of our voices. "We are the lions, the mighty-mighty lions!"

Katie and some others reach up and lower the windows on the bus.

"Everywhere we go, people want to know! *Who* we are, *sooo* we tell them! We are the lions, the mighty-mighty lions!"

We sing louder and louder as we pull into the parking lot next to the soccer fields and see the red shirts of our opponents warming up. When the bus stops, we gather up our soccer gear and walk off together. My heart beats faster with anticipation for the game to come. It's an unsettling but powerful feeling to be with your teammates and enter a strange school where everyone is looking at you as the enemy.

Coach always stresses, "You're representing Clarkstown Middle School, and you'll show class and manners or you won't be playing on this team."

Inside, we politely ask a group of Ramapo students hanging around the halls where the visitor's locker room is so we can put on our cleats and take one last bathroom break before the game. I love the *click-clack-click-clack* sound our cleats make on the rival school's floors—like an advancing army preparing for battle.

Warm-ups remind me of a choreographed dance. Even Jillian would be impressed. First we run the perimeter of the field and feel our opponents' eyes on us, checking out our uniforms, looking for familiar faces from summer camps, and sizing us up. We're not a particularly tall or beefy team, but we're quick, strong, and aggressive. Which explains why we haven't lost a game all season. After we jog our warm-up laps, we break off into the middle of the circle and go through our stretching routine, holding every stretch while we count to ten out loud.

As the co-captains of the team, Katie and I get to go out for the coin toss to see who has possession first. We win the toss—a good sign! Along the sidelines are ball girls wearing their travel soccer team uniforms with matching ribbons in their hair. Bet they're imagining the day when they'll be in middle school playing on this very same field.

Coach calls us into a tight huddle and gives us one last pep talk before the kickoff.

"Be aggressive on the field and fight for every ball. Forwards, take the ball to the goal! Defense, you've got to hunt that ball down! Clear to the outsides and protect our goal!" She puts her right hand in the middle and says, "Let's go—"

We place our hands on top of hers and pump up and down three times, shouting, "Go! Fight! Win!"

Running out onto the field to take our positions, I stop to adjust my nylon soccer socks over my shin guards. From the look on the opposing forward's face, I have a feeling I'm going to be needing them today, big-time.

The ref puts the whistle to her mouth and gives it a sharp blast, and Alison moves the ball forward over the line.

Immediately, Ramapo closes in for the steal. There's no room to maneuver, though, and I lose the ball when #3, a tall, blond, ponytailed girl on offense for Ramapo, kicks the ball out from underneath my feet and takes off with it down the middle of the field.

Coach yells from the sideline, "Chase her down, Munro! You lose it, you dog her until you win that ball back again!"

Hey, it wasn't my intention to lose the ball, Coach! But I guess she has to yell something from the sidelines to let off nervous energy, since she can't be out here on the field winning the game for us.

Katie and Brittany are all over the blond giant, but she's incredibly quick and gets off a shot on goal that just misses going in the upper left corner of our net.

Whew! That was a close one. I check the scoreboard. Only two and a half minutes into the game and I can tell it's going to be the toughest one we've played all year. As Marissa, our goalie, sets up for a goal kick, I see my parents making their way into the stands—Dad in his orange-and-black lion's sweatshirt, and Mom in heels and a suit. I acknowledge them with a quick wave and then position myself so I can make a run for the goal kick coming my way.

At halftime, the score remains 0–0, but the shots on goal tell a different story. Ramapo has twelve to our five.

"What's the matter with you girls today?" demands Coach.

"You need to get your heads in the game!" She slaps the clipboard against her leg. "Too much fooling around on the bus ride over here. Now focus on what needs to be done! You've got to beat them to the ball and control it. If you don't, they'll control the game and win."

We catch our breath as we listen, wiping sweat from our faces with wristbands and drinking cold water from our water bottles.

"You act like you don't know what to do, now that you've come up against an equally aggressive team. You have to want to beat them more than they want to beat you. It's that simple. Now, go out there and do it!"

I hate to see Coach upset. She's one of my favorite adults. Although definitely not the warm and cuddly type, she pushes us to do our best. I don't want to disappoint her and lose our undefeated season, even more than I'd hate to disappoint my own parents.

Ramapo has the kickoff for the start of the second half. The blond bulldozer prepares to receive the pass.

"I've got to score another goal," I say to myself before the whistle blows.

Charging the ball the minute it's tapped over the line, I get my foot in there to break up the play. Frustrated, #3 elbows me hard in the chest. Falling to the ground in pain, I wish I were wearing one of Luke's baseball chest protectors for cheap shots like this one.

The ref waves the yellow card and gives #3 a warning. Our team gets a direct kick from the spot, but it's too far to shoot on goal. We settle for Katie blasting it down the middle, where

I have a footrace with the fullback to get the ball within scoring range. There are not many fullbacks with my speed and finesse, and once I push the ball through the gap in the defense, I'm clear for a breakaway with nothing but the Ramapo goalie in the way of my potential game-winning goal.

She's tall and quick as she races out from between the posts to cut down my angle. I throw a fake with my shoulders, but she doesn't go for it. As I'm about to send the ball into the upper right corner of the net, my legs are swiped out from underneath me and I hit the ground with a disappointing thud. I bang my hand on the ground and curse.

Brittany's yelling, "Foul!"

The ref signals a penalty shot, and Coach indicates that I should take it.

The goalie sets up in the box—hands extended at both sides—nervously shifting her weight from one foot to the other, ready to block my shot.

I know the routine.

I've taken a hundred of these shots in practice, and I try to visualize exactly where I'll send the ball. The goalie's job is much tougher. Basically, she guesses where the shot's going to go and tries to stop it before it crosses the line.

All eyes focus on me as I set the soccer ball on the line and take five steps back to run up on it. I'm confident that I'll make this shot. I know where I'm going to place the ball, and I try not to look at that spot on the net, because right now the goalie is desperately studying my face and body language for clues.

I'm in control. I rarely miss!

The ref blows the whistle.

I run up on the ball with all of my speed and strength con-
verging on that one sweet spot in the middle where my cleat
connects and sends that baby flying forward for the game-
winning goal.

Only the ball never makes it into the net.

The goalie guesses correctly as she dives across the mouth
of the goal, barely grasping the ball and pulling it in close to
her gut, hugging it, victorious, on the ground.

I turn around and cover my face, wishing I could take back
the kick and start all over again. A brief look of disappointment
flickers across Coach's face and then she claps her hands
together and shouts, "Come on girls, forget it! Let's get back
the momentum and put one in the net!"

Katie and Brit put their arms around my shoulders. "It's
okay, Tess. You'll make the next one."

"No, I blew it! I can't believe I missed that shot!"

"Forget it!" Katie says. "It was a good shot. She had a great
save."

In the stands, my parents clap and shout encouragement,
but I can't get over feeling that I've let everyone down. Thank
God, Mark wasn't here. He'd never let me hear the end of it!
And if we lose or tie today—no more bragging to the boy's
team about our undefeated season.

With two minutes left in the game, #3 scores for Ramapo
on an amazing corner kick. With her back to the goal, she
heads the ball into the upper right corner and Marissa can't get
her hands on it in time to stop it from going into the net.

The next 120 seconds pass in slow motion. We have one
last surge toward their goal, but their trash-talking fullbacks

barrel through and clear the ball wide to the outside as time runs out on the clock.

All Coach says after our first loss is, "Go congratulate them and I'll talk to you on the bus."

This year, I've never experienced shaking hands as the losing team after a game. And I don't ever want to do it again—look into the victorious, smiling faces of the enemy and repeat "Good game" over and over again as we halfheartedly slap their hands in a single-file row. I'd rather slap #3's face—only I know it's just being a sore loser on my part. I hate feeling this way—jealous and angry.

Soccer Chick Rule Number 5 – Losing sucks!

On the bus ride home, everyone is silent. No singing or laughing. No eating candy or cupcakes. No iPods. No fun.

Coach waits until we pull up in front of the school before standing up and saying, "Sometimes there's more to be learned in losing than in winning. Now it's our job to find out what the lesson is. I know it doesn't feel too good right now. But I promise you we'll work on our weak areas and improve. And we're lucky to have the opportunity to play them again before the season's over—at home!"

I thought about what Coach said during the game about being distracted and not focusing. I thought I was focused on the goal, but then I missed. I hope no one blames me. I hope I can stop blaming myself.

⚽ CHAPTER EIGHT

"Why should it be up to people who don't go to school anymore to decide if we have sports or not?" I ask Mom.

She checks the vegetable lasagna in the microwave and pulls off the plastic covering. "Because property taxes are how most public schools are financed. You have to vote on them."

"What if we lose?"

She resets the microwave. "Tess, why the doubt all of a sudden? When you and Bo signed up all those people for yard signs, you were confident that you'd win. This have anything to do with the soccer game the other day?"

I shrug and grab a carrot from the salad. "I don't know—maybe. I thought we were the best. That we could beat any team in our league. I never missed a penalty shot like that before. Maybe I've misjudged our chances of winning the levy, too, and then we'll lose sports."

"Tess, in Cleveland, levies have failed for years. Forget sports—students are in classrooms that aren't heated in the winter, ceilings caving in, water damage. No textbooks, desks, basic school supplies."

I sigh. This sounds like her clean-your-plate-children-are-starving-in-India speech. "Okay, Mom. But it still su—stinks if we lose. I can't imagine going to school and not staying after for sports. I mean, what's the point?"

Mom looks up from chopping veggies and gives me a stern

look, and I wonder, did progress reports come in the mail today?

"I understand how you feel." She walks over to the fridge and opens the door. "Did your father pick up some milk the other day?"

"In the back. Behind the orange juice."

"Hey, what's for dinner?" Mark stops the microwave and opens the door for a peek.

"Reset that and be patient!" says Mom.

"Mark, tomorrow after school, could you drive Bo and me around so we can put up the yard signs for the levy?"

"Nope, I'm busy." He grabs a breadstick from the table and shoves it in his mouth.

"It won't take long. Mom and Dad have a dinner, and Bo's mom works late on Fridays."

Mom gives Mark a lawyerly stare. Unlike Dad, she has no problem playing judge, jury, and jailer in our lives. Since Mark's on probation for the mailbox mishap, I know she's thinking that he should do his civic duty and lend a hand for a good cause.

Mom doesn't say a word—one look, and Mark gets the message loud and clear.

"All right, all right, I'll drive you and goalie boy around for an hour, but that's it!

"Just be quick and pitch the dumb signs out the car windows because I'm not wasting my Friday night with you two!"

"Thanks, Mark." I try planting a big kiss on his face, but he grumpily grabs another breadstick and retreats to his room until dinner.

Friday in school, Bo gets in trouble during lunch for trying to
juggle two apples and an orange. But a girl fight distracts the
monitors and they forget to assign him a detention. A pack of
eighth-grade girls targets a few pretty sixth-grade girls who
need to be put back in their place.

The principal breaks up the fight and practically carries
one of the hysterical eighth-grade girls out of the cafeteria in a
bear hug. Everyone else is hyped and chanting, "Fight, fight,
fight!"

Ibby says, "I hate it when they act like this—animals. Why
do they like to see people fight?"

"Don't know," I say. "I guess it's like reality TV in front of
their faces." I try to distract her. "Hey, my mom said you could
sleep over tonight. After school today, Bo and I are putting up
the levy signs. Want to help?"

"Sure, but how are you going to carry all those signs?"

"Mark's going to drive us around."

"Oh." Ibby takes a sip from her water bottle. "Maybe I'll
meet you at your house after you're done."

"Come with us, Ibs. It'll be fun."

"I'm not allowed in the car if Mark's driving—remember?"

"Oops, forgot." This summer, when Mark first got his
temps, he drove Ibby home after a visit. When he dropped her
off, he accidentally drove up onto their lawn and crushed one
of Mrs. Bloom's antique garden gnomes. She added *teen driv-
ers* to her list of phobias and made a rule that Ibby wouldn't be

allowed to drive with Mark from then on. I offer her a barbeque potato chip. "Meet you at my house after, then. Say, around seven or so. Okay?"

She takes two chips. "Sure, thanks."

In Discovery Tech, Mrs. Bustamonte's in a better mood today. Sarah Willingham apparently went around the school and collected every last mouse ball she could find. She put them in a juice-box purse that she stitched together herself from used plastic juice packets and presented them to Mrs. B.

Some people have way too much time on their hands.

Mr. Metz is not in a good mood. The word around school is that Georgie's parents complained about him to the principal. Metz was forced to attend a meeting and listen to the Taxuses' ideas on how he should teach intelligent design in Science, along with evolution.

I heard that they also brought up Bo's Pledge of Allegiance and encouraged the school to take disciplinary action against him for disrespecting both God and country. I hope Mrs. Korn explained to them that it's nothing personal. And besides, Bo's the only kid I know who can recite extensive passages from the Bible as well as Lincoln's Emancipation Proclamation—by heart.

When I get home from school, the levy signs and their metal posts have been delivered and are stacked in a neat pile next to my garage door—all fifty-three of them. Wow! Somehow seeing the slogan INVEST IN THE BEST on a little orange-and-black schoolhouse drives it all home. This is it! People really will be going to the polls next week to vote. Bo and I have our work cut out for us this afternoon to get these up in the neighborhood.

I begin by slipping the placard signs over the metal posts and stapling the sides together. I'm just about finished when Bo walks up the driveway and says, "Hey, you didn't tell me we had to make them!"

"I'm not making them, only stapling them together so we can put them in the ground. See, the wire posts and the signs come separately."

"'Invest in the best'?" he reads out loud. "What a load of crap!"

I shrug. "You've got to sell it or they won't vote for it."

Bo walks into the garage. "What's with the little orange schoolhouse with the bell on top? Since when do schools look like that? Would've been better if they put an armed guard in a tower." He comes out holding a basketball, bounces it twice, puts it through his legs, and then takes a jump shot. It bounces off the rim and begins rolling down the driveway into the street.

"Hey!" I shout. "Feel free to pitch in anytime."

"Got to get ready. Basketball tryouts in three weeks." He retrieves the ball and continues dribbling past an imaginary defense, up and down the driveway.

"Not going to be any tryouts if the levy doesn't pass."

"Right!" Bo tosses the ball onto the lawn and picks up a sign and jabs it into the ground. "There, don't say I didn't do my part."

"Nice try—hey, watch out!"

Speeding down the street, Mark makes a sharp turn into our driveway—barely missing the replacement mailbox Dad put up just three days ago. He guns the car, pretending to run us over, and stops with a squeal of brakes five feet in front of us.

"Your brother's a maniac."

"Tell me about it. Ibby's not allowed to get in the car with him, otherwise she'd be here helping us."

"Lucky Ibs."

Slamming the car door, Mark says, "Hey, losers, if you want me to chauffer your lazy butts around, you'd better load all those signs in the trunk by the time I come back out or you can forget about it!"

He steps over the posts I'm trying to untangle. "Tess, almost as much metal here as in your mouth."

I jab at him with a post, but he leaps out of the way and slams the garage door behind him.

"Friendly guy," Bo mutters.

"He's gotten worse ever since he got his license and Luke left for college. Pretty soon, he's going to need a convertible because his big fat ego won't fit in this car."

Bo and I count out the signs—forty-one of them. We leave the twelve extra leaning against the side of the garage and gather up the rest to put in the trunk. We've just about got them in when we hear a familiar voice behind us. "Hello there!"

What is she doing here?

I don't think Jillian's been on this side of the street since she moved in this summer. Did she come over to get a levy sign? I tried two more times to talk to her parents, and every time I rang the bell, Jillian answered and said that they weren't home or that they couldn't come to the door. Yeah, right. She's just jerking me around.

Bo says, "Hey, Jillian. What's up?"

"*My* dance troupe just won a major competition and now *I'm* heading for Regionals next week. *I'm* so excited because *I* did most of the choreography and *I* designed the costumes as well. *I* think *I* have a great shot at winning the whole competition!"

And *I* think Jillian has a pronoun problem.

"Cool," says Bo, and he makes a fist and gently knocks his knuckles against hers in congratulations.

"Jillian, we're putting up yard signs." I look at her knowingly. "Which reminds me—"

"I know. I know," Jillian says, waving her purple nails in my face. "Mark asked me to come over."

I glare at the house, looking for my Benedict Arnold brother.

Jillian continues, "We're catching an early movie at the cineplex and he figures it would save time if we did the signs on the way."

We?

I must look like a fish in Mark's aquarium. The one whose big mouth repeatedly opens and closes but nothing comes out of it. Mark and Jillian O'Hanlon on a date? What happened to hating the O'Hanlons? Why complicate things by turning her into a girlfriend?

On cue, Mark walks out of the garage. I notice he's wearing that expensive T-shirt again, and he reeks of aftershave or some stinky cologne. Has he totally lost his mind over this fluff chick?

Everyone piles into the car except me. I stand there in back of the trunk, wondering if it's too late to pull all the signs out and maybe find another ride. Mark turns the key, and exhaust fumes hit my face. I slam the trunk and quickly move out of the way. With Mark's driving record, I'm in danger of becoming driveway-kill.

"Wait, I forgot the clipboard with the addresses!" I shout. I run into the garage and grab them from the workbench.

Of course, Mark doesn't wait.

He throws the car into reverse, tires squealing, as he just misses the new mailbox for the second time, and peals out into the street. There, he drives along close to the sidewalk at about five miles per hour. The three of them laugh their heads off in the car as I run to catch up.

"It's not funny, Mark!" I shout, smacking the window with my hand.

But I guess it is, because he doesn't stop until we're about fifty yards from our home. I yank open the door. "You skipped three houses that need signs, moron!"

"More fun watching you run!"

"Pop the trunk before I pop your face!"

I pull the first sign out and furiously stab it into the Stimpsons' front lawn. When I get back into the car, Jillian's got the radio blasting as she sings along with the pop music and does slutty dance moves with her upper body in the front seat. Mark's laughing, and Bo's bouncing around the backseat, mocking her big-time.

"Get this dance on," Jillian sings.

"Get these *signs* up!" I shout over the radio. "How about one for your house, Jillian?"

She shimmies. She shakes. She shuns me.

We spent the next hour and a half stop and go, rap, R&B, rock and roll, up and down the streets of our neighborhood, until every last sign is on a front lawn. Mark drops Bo off at a friend's house, and I assume he'll take me home to meet Ibby. Instead, he claims they're running late for the movie and would I mind if he let me out right here, three blocks from home?

I could make a huge scene and threaten to accompany them to the movie if they don't drive me home, but the thought of spending another minute with these two makes me want to puke. I bail out of the car, slam the door, and start jogging home. I feel like I could run a marathon if I had to.

⚽

"I can't believe your brother would date Jillian," says Ibby later that night as we share a bowl of popcorn and watch one of our favorite Jane Austen films, *Pride and Prejudice*. "I mean, from everything you've told me, they're total opposites. It doesn't make sense."

"Nooo, they're exactly the same," I say. "Both jerks!"

Ibby laughs and licks the salt and butter from her fingers. "Well, then they deserve each other. Poetic justice, as Mr. Chen always says."

"I guess, but it burns me up about the signs. She acts so fake and nice to the boys, but treats me like dirt. She wouldn't even let me talk to her parents. I know it's only one vote, but I hate the fact that she thinks she's won!"

"She hasn't won, Tess. Voters will decide on November second."

"Unless . . ."

"Oh, no. There's that I've-got-a-plan look in your eyes again."

"Remember those extra signs I told you about?"

"Yes, but—"

"Wouldn't it be a shame for them to go to waste?"

"Tess, I don't think—"

I grab her hand and pull her toward the door. "No time for thinking, Ibs. Time for action!"

There's something really eerie about being outside at two o'clock in the morning when everyone in your neighborhood, including your parents and dorky brother, have long gone to bed. The air is cold and we can see our breath. The grass crunches when we walk on it, stiff with the first frost finally blanketing our town. About a dozen signs are leaning against the side of the garage where I left them. I grab three and head down the driveway.

Ibby stands there in red flannel cat pajamas and flip-flops. "Tess," she whispers.

"Huh?"

"What are you doing? Jillian didn't say *yes* to even one sign on her lawn."

"Yeah, I know." The metal posts are cold so I shift them to my other hip. "But, she didn't say *no* to three."

Ibs nervously runs her hands through her curly hair and sighs. She knows there's no talking me out of it, so the best she can do is to follow me across the street and try to be a voice of reason in the middle of the night.

I stick the first sign right smack in the middle of a dandelion patch and put the other two on either side—INVEST IN THE BEST, INVEST IN THE BEST, INVEST IN THE BEST!

"Beautiful," I whisper.

Ibby stands there with her arms crossed, shaking her head disapprovingly. "Okay, you've made your point—three times. Now, let's go back inside. I'm freezing."

"Not yet."

"You're trespassing. You're going to get in trouble!" she hisses.

I sling my arm across her shoulders and step back, admiring my work. "Chill, Ibs."

"No problem," she mutters, "I'm freezing my ass off."

I laugh out loud, covering my mouth so as not to wake the O'Hanlons.

Ibby smiles, beginning to enjoy the fun of letting a curse word fly in the dead of night while standing in the middle of the road in flip-flops and flannel.

"We're not going to get in any trouble, and even if we did, wouldn't it be worth it to see the expression on Jillian's face?"

Ibby smiles. "I guess so."

We hear a noise from across the street.

"Oh no!"

The garage door to my house opens and a dark figure stands silhouetted in front of the light for a moment, closes the door, and makes his way down the driveway.

"*Now* I'm in trouble," I say.

"What are you two losers doing out here in the middle of the night? Halloween's not for another—*whoa!*" He points to the signs on the O'Hanlons' lawn. "You do that?" he demands.

Ibby looks at me wide-eyed. Having grown up an only child with a timid cat, she's failed to develop a healthy disregard for an older brother's stupid questions.

"You're in deep freakin' trouble, Tess Munro! Don't you know it's against the law to put political signs on people's front lawns without their permission? You want Mom to lose her license? Dad, his job at the school?"

Ibby's shoulders tremble beside me.

"You're full of crap, Mark! No one's going to lose their job. Besides, it's *my* job to put up the signs in this neighborhood, so go back to bed with your Woo-woo doggie and your shabby-lookin' boxers and mind your own business!"

"Woo-woo doggie?" whispers Ibby.

"A stuffed animal he's been sleeping with since he was a baby," I explain.

"Okay, crazy girl. Psycho sis." He takes a couple of jabs at my face, stopping just short of contact.

I brace myself and refuse to back down.

"But don't say I didn't warn you when we're tossed out onto the street this winter, huddled around a barrel fire, toasting marshmallows and wienies stuck on your stupid metal signposts."

I shake my head. "You're the one who's toasted, Mark. Come on, Ibs." Grabbing hold of her icy hand, I lead her back toward the house, with Mark grumbling behind us. In the pitch-black garage, we almost trip over a pile of sneakers and a basketball lying on the floor in front of the door.

A fierce whisper—"Hey!"

We turn around.

"Where you going?" Mark asks, as he absentmindedly scratches the waistband of his boxers.

"Inside, dorko."

"You got to finish the job." And with that, Mark lifts the remaining nine signs leaning against the garage and carries them across the street. They rattle and clank against each other as they hit his leg. Ibby and I watch in amazement as, one by one, he plants them in the ground all over the O'Hanlons' front yard.

"Tess?"

"Hmm?"

"How do you think Mark's date with Jillian O'Hanlon went tonight?"

"I don't know." I smile at her. "But I think it's safe to say that there probably wasn't any good-night kiss!"

CHAPTER NINE

At soccer practice on Monday, Katie juggles the soccer ball in front of me.

"So what did"—head ball–thigh—"the cop"—left foot–right—"say"—thigh–thigh—"when he came"—right foot–left—"to your door?"

"'Good morning, Patricia.'"

"What!" Katie stops juggling and catches the ball in her arms.

"He knew my mother from court." I yank the long shoelaces on my cleats, wrap the excess around the bottom, and tie them with a double knot on top. "Two months ago, she represented the cop's brother in a custody battle."

Katie whistles and begins juggling the soccer ball again. "So, did he give your mom a ticket or something?"

"Nope—just laughed when she told him what had probably happened. Then, he turned to me and told my mom to keep an eye on me—I looked like a handful."

"That's so cool, Tess. You didn't get in any trouble!"

"Oh, I did—probably would have gotten off easier if the cop punished me instead of Judge Mom. Now I'm stuck weeding the O'Hanlons' stupid lawn all next weekend, writing a letter of apology explaining my momentary lapse of sanity, and collecting their mail when they go out of town during Thanksgiving break."

"Well, at least it's the end of the season. How many weeds can they actually have this time of year?"

I finish tying the second cleat and grab a soccer ball from inside Coach's mesh bag. "Katie, you have no idea."

The whistle blows and Coach calls us over to talk strategy before we get down to work. We lean on each other and continue stretching while she draws with her dry-erase pen on a clipboard.

"Here's where we're getting beat every time. They draw our backs out to the sides and send their strongest girl up the middle for the crossing pass."

A picture of the tall blond striker, #3, pops into my head. I frown and block the setting sun with my hand to study Coach's Xs and Os in front of me.

"Pay attention! These aren't hugs and kisses, girls. With number three's foot skills and speed, it wasn't difficult for her to get a shot off. We have to contain their offense and put someone on her at all times to shut her down! I want someone who's tough and can hassle the hell out of her every time she comes near the ball! Do you hear me?" asks Coach, slapping the clipboard with her hand.

My heart pounds in my chest. I know I'm the fastest on the team and I'm definitely one of the more aggressive players. But I'm a forward and wouldn't usually come all the way back to help out on defense. I remember that look of triumph on #3's face after she scored the winning goal, and how good it feels to slap hands on the winning side at the end of the game.

"I'll do it," I say. "I'll mark number three."

Coach smiles. "That's exactly what I had in mind, Tess. Thanks for stepping up to the plate.

"Okay, let's get to work. We play Ramapo again on November second, our very last game of the season, and this time, let's win!"

Dribbling the ball down to the goal for a two-on-three shooting drill, I wonder why that date sounds familiar. Then, it hits me. November 2 is Election Day! Late that night or early the next morning, we'll know whether we have sports next season, and whether I should even bother getting out of bed to come to school.

Mark picks me up after practice because Mom's working late again and Dad has a meeting. He's uncharacteristically quiet on the drive home. No music blaring, two hands on the wheel, eyes on the road, careful driving. It's totally freaking me out.

"Mark, are you still fighting with Jillian?"

"Nope, going out this Friday. Some Halloween dance at her school."

"So, she forgives you for the yard signs?"

"Nope."

"Then why is she going out with you?"

"Told her you did it."

I hit him on the arm and then remember that that's probably not a good idea while he's driving. "Hey, I'll take the blame for the first three, buddy, but not all twelve!"

Mark just nods mechanically as we turn onto our street. Immediately, I notice that something's different. It's like, you know your home turf so well that if neighbors change their landscaping or paint their house a different color, it jumps right out at you.

The large sign erected on the O'Hanlons' front lawn doesn't just jump out at me. It's a full-body blow that hits me in the gut and knocks the wind out of me. Mark turns into our driveway and I twist around in the seat, gaping at the monstrosity.

"What are they doing?" I scream, pounding the dashboard with my hand.

"What?" Mark feigns innocence.

He's a lousy actor.

"That's what! That sign!" I point across the street. "They're not allowed to do that!"

He turns the car off and sighs. "Actually, they are. It's their property. They can do whatever they want."

"It's not fair. If they don't want to vote for the levy, they don't have to. But don't campaign against it! It's nasty and mean and after all our hard work. . . ." Tears well up in my eyes, and I wipe them with the sleeve of my sweatshirt.

I wait for the abuse.

Surprisingly, Mark doesn't call me a big crybaby or tell me that it's my fault for sticking the pro-levy signs on their lawn in the first place. Instead, he grabs my backpack, opens his door, and says, "Come on, Tess, let's go eat dinner."

I refuse to follow him in. I stand at the end of the driveway, staring at the four-foot square plywood sign looming over my puny INVEST IN THE BEST on our front lawn.

The O'Hanlon sign is lettered in purple on a white background and reads:

ON NOVEMBER 2ND VOTE NO TO HIGHER TAXES!

At the bottom, there's a small box with a checkmark in it and the word "NO!"

My vision blurs in purple and white—St. Jude's school colors and the color of Jillian's nails! I want to run over there and kick it down. I want to spray-paint graffiti all over the stupid sign—liars!

At the end of my driveway, underneath the bushes, is an old soccer ball that must have rolled out of my garage. I pull it out from under the branches, brush off a few soggy leaves, and tee it up on my front lawn. Running on it with all my pent-up fury and frustration, I pretend that it's Jillian O'Hanlon's head.

Thwak!

The ball flies across the street and hits the sign with a satisfying *wump* and then ricochets right back at me. The sign wobbles a little but doesn't fall.

Mark leans out our front door. "Come on, Tess. I'm making cheese macaroni!"

Only then do I know just how bad the situation is. Cheese macaroni is my favorite. The last time Mark was this nice, I'd fallen out of our tree fort in the backyard and broken my arm.

CHAPTER TEN

Vice Principal Korn likes to say over the PA that we're one big, happy Clarkstown Lions family. There's no doubt, though, that we have a few dysfunctional members in the pride.

Georgie Taxus leaves the classroom in science. Not because he's protesting Metz's teaching. This time, it's totally Georgie's fault. But I bet he won't tell it that way to the nurse or to his parents when he gets home.

In Metz's room, there's an aquarium with a hamster named Calypso. Most days, Calypso is too sleepy to bother with any of us. Occasionally, she comes out of her shredded-toilet-paper-tube nest, eats a few seeds or carrot sticks, and goes for a spin on her exercise wheel. About once a month, Metz puts Calypso in a clear exercise ball and she rolls around the classroom floor underneath our lab desks, getting caught behind the garbage can, computer wires, and filing cabinets.

Although she's called a teddy bear hamster, don't let that fool you. Calypso's not the warm-and-cuddly type. She hates middle school kids, especially Joey Montanado, Chris Abrams, and Georgie Taxus, all of whom take pleasure—when Metz is not looking—in poking pencils into Calypso's cage, dropping pennies on her nest, and giving her plastic globe a quick push with their feet whenever she trundles by.

When Metz is late for class today, Georgie reaches his hand into the tank and tries to wake Calypso for a spin on her wheel.

Hamsters never forgive—or forget.

With a flash of her yellowed incisors, Calypso chomps down on Georgie's right index finger and refuses to let go. There's blood and a lot of high-pitched screaming before Georgie convinces Calypso that his finger is not a carrot stick.

"Whoa! You're gonna need a rabies shot now," warns Joey, "and the needle's three feet long—right in your gut—ugh!" He stabs his stomach and collapses over his desk, twitching.

Georgie's face is blotchy and his eyes begin to water.

Olivia hands him Kleenex. "People can die from rabies, you know."

With a wad of red-soaked tissues bunched around the wound, Georgie's just about to lose it, when Metz walks in the door. "She bit me for no reason!" Georgie cries.

Metz looks confused. "Olivia?"

"No! Calypso."

"Whew! That's better. People actually have more germs in their mouths than hamsters. Go down to the nurse and get it cleaned out, George."

He's almost out the door when Metz asks, "By the way, how did your hand come in contact with Calypso's teeth?"

Georgie's face turns even redder and he shrugs. "Don't know . . . she just bit me."

"Hmm," says Metz. He peers into the tank as Calypso takes refuge under the cedar chips.

Later that day in Phys Ed, everyone teases Georgie. Nurse Bicknell went a little overboard with the gauze, and it's wrapped about an inch thick around his entire hand and halfway up his arm.

"Hey, mummy, Halloween's not 'til Friday!" Joey calls.

Pretending to box, Bo takes a couple of fake jabs at Georgie's head.

Olivia insists on signing it with a red marker. It bleeds into the gauze, making it look like the wound has opened up, which causes Mr. Wadler to send Georgie back down to the nurse's office for rebandaging.

"Tell her to do your whole body this time," Joey says.

Georgie tries to give him the finger, but all he can manage is a lame mummy wave.

We turn our attention to Mr. Wadler and wait to find out what it'll be today. A hush falls over the gymnasium.

Wadler crosses his arms over his barrel chest, scratches his beard, and speaks the two most beautiful words in a gym teacher's vocabulary: "Battle ball."

High fives and joyous whoops break out among the athletically gifted, while Olivia Fletcher stomps her feet and whines, "Not again!" and Ibby calculates where she has to stand in order to wind up on Bo's or my team.

There's no other game in Phys Ed quite so pure, simple, and vicious. Kickball doesn't even come close. Badminton—a game for girls who grew up on Beanie Babies and Barbies.

With battle ball, it's survival of the swift and strong. It's a fierce athletic competition where there's no mercy and nowhere to hide. The winners exult in bragging rights for the remainder of the day. The losers pray not to get nailed in the head or other, ah, sensitive areas.

After counting off by twos, Bo, Ibby, and I wind up on the same team. My heart races as we line up on either side of the basketball court in the gym, waiting for Wadler to blow the whistle and roll the six rubber balls out onto the floor so the game can begin. But Wadler always goes over all the rules, even though we've heard them a hundred times before. I guess he feels he wouldn't be doing his job if he didn't read us the battle ball bill of rights.

"You have the right to throw the ball, without crossing the mid-court line, and hit someone anywhere on their body. If you hit them, then they're out of the game. But if they catch the ball you threw, you're out."

We know, we know. I retie my sneakers impatiently. Some teachers are madly in love with the sound of their own voices.

"If you nail someone in the head without them ducking first, then you're out.

But if you nail them in the head and they've had the chance to duck, then *they're* out.

You have the right to shoot at the other team's basketball hoop, and if it goes in, then anyone who's out on your team gets to come back into the game and you're a hero. . . ."

I glance at Bo, who is rocking back and forth on his feet, catlike, ready to get this game started. *Come on, Wadler!* I scream in my brain. Let's play the game.

Miraculously, Wadler puts the whistle up to his mouth and is just about to give it a blast when Georgie walks into the gym. The wound's rewrapped with clean gauze and he's wearing one of Nurse Bicknell's infamous latex gloves. He waves at us with his white cartoon-character hand. Wadler declares him fit for combat, throws him on our team, and blasts the whistle.

Bo and I immediately charge to center court, careful not to

go over the line as we scoop up three of the six battle balls. Joey Montanado and Chris Abrams do the same for their team.

Whoosh! A ball comes whizzing by my head and smacks against the orange mats along the back wall. Ibby scrambles for it.

Bo charges out to mid-court, wielding the red rubber ball high above his head. Intimidated, the other team backs up and crouches low for the catch, even though they know that, with Bo's strength, their chances are slim to none that they'll be able to hold on to it.

Bo lets it fly—*wham!* It nails Chris Abrams in the shoulder. Chris makes a grab for it, but the ball ricochets off his arm and hits two other people before bouncing across the court. All three are out.

"Yes!" Bo and I exchange high fives.

I whip my ball at Olivia, who's standing in the back row gossiping with Zoey Garcia. Olivia doesn't even attempt to catch the ball as it smacks off her leg. Sticking her tongue out at me, she walks off the court to sit in the bleachers with Wadler and the rest of the people who are out.

All the battle balls, except the one Ibby clutches in her hands, are on the other side now. Joey organizes his teammates in a coordinated attack against Bo. They charge up to the half-court line and pummel their target.

Using his amazing goalie skills, Bo leaps, twists, and tries to dodge the assault. But Joey Montanado hits Bo on the side of the head and Wadler rules Bo out, along with two of our other players who were caught in the line of fire.

I scramble to retrieve the loose balls on our side and toss

another one to Ibs. Meanwhile, far from the action, Georgie amuses himself with the latex glove by blowing it up with air. The ballooned glove looks like a cow's udder as Georgie bops it all around, oblivious to the battle being waged all around him.

"Hey, Georgie, we could use a little help here. We're getting killed!" I toss him a ball and tell him to try and distract the other team so I can get close enough to make a basket and get everyone on our team back in the game. It's our only hope.

Ibs understands the plan and runs to the far side of our court, taunting Joey and friends. A ball comes flying at her but she uses the two balls in her arms as shields and knocks the opposing team's ball away.

Georgie's idea of a distraction is to hold the ballooned glove on top of his head and run around *cock-a-doodle-do*ing like some psycho rooster. I have to give him credit. It definitely gets their attention. Joey and company attack with a vengeance.

I check the clock on the gym wall. The bell's going to ring in one minute. They're up five players to our three—oops—make that two. Georgie got nailed in the nuts.

Joey reads my intentions. Scooping up a ball rolling in front of him, he prepares to throw it at me or knock my shot off-course if I try for their basket.

Ibby, who hates to throw the ball because the boys tease her and say she "throws like a girl," throws one—like a girl—at Joey's head in order to keep him from blocking my potential game-winning three-pointer.

Bo's shouting and stomping the wooden bleachers, and Olivia's forgotten her gossip and just sits there screaming, "Get Tess out! Hit Tess!"

I line up my shot. No time for BEEF. Just a quick—release!

The ball arcs high above my opponents' heads. My body braces for the hits that are about to come, since I'm out at mid-court—exposed and alone. But I can't take my eyes off the ball. Sometimes, you just have a feeling that it's going in and you have to watch no matter . . .

Thwak! Whomp-wham!

I see shooting bright lights and, for a minute, I'm confused as to why my hands are touching the gym floor. An explosion of sound breaks in my head as Bo, Ibby, and the rest of my teammates pull me up off the floor and slap my back in cele-bration.

My face throbs with pain, and there's an angry red imprint from the texture of the battle ball on one of my cheeks. Even though I missed watching my shot until the very end—the bas-ket was good. We won the battle-ball game today in gym, and it was *sooo* worth it!

Soccer Chick Rule Number 6 – Sometimes you've got to take one for the team.

CHAPTER ELEVEN

Everyone knows that Halloween at Clarkstown Middle School is basically permission for some girls to celebrate Dress-Like-a-Slut Day. Olivia and friends decide to dress as angels. I use "dress" in the loosest terms. We're not talking Old Testament, white-robed, harp-strumming, heavenly angels. We're talking push-up bra, belly-baring, barely dressed angels.

Mrs. Korn announces over the PA that teachers should send students with costumes of a questionable nature down to the office during homeroom. The principal will rule on whether it's a dress code violation or not. If they have a rule about wearing underwear as outerwear to school, there're going to be a lot of violations today.

I keep it simple and wear my soccer uniform to school with a sign that says "Mia" on the front and a picture of a ham on the back—my favorite player! Bo doesn't make it past first period before Mrs. Bustamonte adjusts her glasses, clears her throat, and sends him down to the office. He protests her call. "What? I'm fully dressed and surrounded by a cardboard box!" he insists.

"To the office!"

"Aw, come on, Mrs. B.! It took me three days to make this. I painted it and everything."

Unmoved, Mrs. B. stands at the door, shaking her head and pointing the way down the hall. "Out!"

"It's a public health message," Bo insists as he gathers up his books, bumps between the rows of desks, and high-fives his friends all the way to the door. He turns and gives us one last look at the offending costume, supposedly inspired by his mom's job at a radiologist's office.

It's a cardboard box, the kind used for large appliances, with two circular holes, about the size of grapefruits, cut out of the cardboard in front, just below a rectangular opening for Bo's face.

A sign above Bo's head reads, *Mammograms.* An arrow pointing to the circular holes reads, *Insert breasts here.*

"Let the principal be the judge. Personally, I think it's sexual harassment. Aren't any of you young ladies offended?"

I don't have the heart to tell Mrs. B. that breasts sell everything from cars to teen magazines. We wouldn't know to be offended if size triple-Ds were staring us in the face. Some of us just hope we'll develop our own before we go to high school next fall and finally have something to fill out the sports bras we've been wearing since third grade.

"Go Taubs!" calls Joey Montanado.

"At least *you* picked an appropriate costume, Joey," says Mrs. B. She closes the classroom door and walks over to her desk to take attendance. Scanning the rows for empty seats, she says, "A circus clown. Now, that's a cute idea—especially since everyone loves balloons. Can you blow them up and twist them into little balloon animals like they used to do when I was a little girl?"

The class cracks up.

"He's not a *balloon* clown, Mrs. B.," smirks Olivia, who is forced to wear a smelly, oversized T-shirt from the school Lost and Found because the principal ruled her costume obscene. "Those are rubbers glued to his sweats."

Mrs. B.'s back stiffens; she stops taking attendance and peers over her glasses at Joey. "Prophylactics?"

Olivia nods. "Condoms."

After her coughing fit subsides, Mrs. B. says, "Joey, why don't you gather up your things and join your friend Mr. Tauber at the office?"

Joey borrows a page from Bo's playbook: "Condoms save lives!"

Georgie whines, "I thought this was Discovery Tech, not Health. If you keep talking about condoms, Mrs. B., I have my mother's permission to go to Industrial Arts, where I can learn something constructive. Abstinence is all they taught at my old school."

"And on what planet was that? Mars?" asks Olivia.

"Akron, Ohio—rubber capital of the world."

"Did you say *rubber*?"

"As in, Goodyear," he says. "Number one supplier of NASCAR champions for the third straight—"

"That'll be enough, George," says Mrs. B. "Now, class, turn on your computers and take out your textbooks. We're on lesson—"

"Mrs. B." Olivia raises her hand and holds her computer mouse up for Mrs. B.'s inspection. "Look!"

Mrs. B.'s glasses slip off her nose for the third time today.

Another mouse ball bites the dust.

"*Hellooo,* shoes!" I whisper to Ibby in the media center during tenth-period study hall as I point to the librarian's costume.

Our librarian is dressed as a Dutch girl with a white wimpled hat, blue-and-white skirt, and authentic wooden clogs. I don't mind when teachers get into the holidays, but sometimes their sense of humor is a bit wacko. Like Nurse Bicknell dressing as a vampire and scheduling a teachers' Red Cross blood drive for this afternoon or Mrs. Korn in a prison jumpsuit with a Styrofoam ball and chain fastened to her leg.

In order to communicate, Ibby and I write in my notebook and pass it back and forth to each other so we don't get thrown out of the library for talking. But we've written less than half a page when we're asked, "Young ladies, are you getting your work done?"

Work? All day today, teachers have been handing out candy in class. Not to mention the stuff we brought from home and ate for lunch, even though our parents tried to hide it for the trick-or-treaters tomorrow night. By now, we're so stoked on sugar that we can't shut up or sit still, and a few of us are acting downright crazy. Ibby and I are busy mapping out the path people will take through the haunted house, when I feel something sting the back of my neck.

"Ouch!" A piece of candy corn hits my arm and lands on my notebook.

Bo and his buddies point and laugh.

"Knock it off!" I whisper.

Another piece sails across the room.

Bo holds the distinction of having been kicked out of the library this year more than any other kid in the entire school. I think he's shooting for the all-time record, held by Marty Mikulsky, who was famous for slipping magazines in unsuspecting students' backpacks, causing the theft alarm to ring repeatedly as people filed out of the library for their next class.

Bo has issues with the librarian because she hesitates to let him take books out. It might be the eighteen dollars he owes in overdue fines, but I think it goes deeper than that. She's protective and looks at the books sort of like children—little book babies. Based on his rowdy behavior in the library, maybe she's afraid if she allows them to hang out with Bo Tauber, they won't come back and behave themselves by sitting in neat little rows on the library shelves.

She approaches Bo's table and whispers, "I'm afraid I'm going to have to ask you to leave now, Mr. Tauber."

Bo, who was stripped of his mobile mammogram unit at the office, pleads, "I have to do research on the Napoleonic period for Social Studies. Please don't kick me out. I promise I won't fool around anymore!"

Maybe she thinks that Bo doesn't appreciate books or history because he's always fooling around. I bet she'd be surprised to know that he watches the History Channel every night and has read all of Michael Shaara's Civil War novels. Even a goalie's got to have a hobby.

"Sorry, you've lost your chance for today, and now you'll have to leave."

Maybe it's the fact that this is the second class Bo was kicked out of today—Metz nailed him for putting dissected

worms in the water fountain—or maybe it's the disappointment at not being able to wear his costume or maybe you can
just blame it on a sugar overdose, but Bo doesn't leave right
away. Instead, he throws his backpack on the floor by Ibby's
feet and sits down next to me at our table.

"Hey, what's up?"

"Thanks a lot for the candy corn," I say. "Next time, warn
me before you pitch them and I'll open my mouth and give you
a target."

"Here, you want some?" He reaches into his sweatshirt
pocket and grabs a handful.

"No food in the library! And I believe, Mr. Tauber, you were
asked to leave."

"I'm going!" Bo gathers up his backpack and heads for the
exit, but before he makes it through the door, the security
alarm sounds, the boys' table goes crazy laughing, and Bo is
called back to the desk for a backpack search.

A library magazine for cat lovers is confiscated from Bo's
backpack.

"I swear I didn't take it. I've been framed! I don't even like
cats!"

"Here, kitty, kitty, kitty!" Joey Montanado calls.

The magazine looks familiar. I give Ibby a knowing smile.

"Meow," she says. "Trick or treat!"

⚽ CHAPTER TWELVE

It rains before practice begins this afternoon, but as long as the lightning sensor doesn't sound, we're expected to be on the field by three. At the end of the season, there's more mud than grass on the field. I love mud soccer!

It would be different if it were cool and still raining, but it's humid and the late October sun warms our faces as we run laps around the field. Only two more practices before our last game, and I want to enjoy every last minute.

Coach blows her whistle and outlines her goals for today's practice.

"I want you to concentrate. Focus on what we've been working on all week. If you practice hard today and Monday, on Tuesday against Ramapo, all that you've worked on will come naturally to you."

We listen and lean against each other, stretching out our leg and back muscles.

Placing her hand in the middle of our huddle, Coach says, "Everyone in."

Each player places her hand on top of the others. "Go, fight, win—*team!*" we shout in unison and break for ball drills.

At first it's awkward and slippery trying to maneuver on a muddy field. Fortunately, our cleats offer some traction, and soon we develop a touch for how far the ball will roll in these conditions. I'm glad the game on Tuesday will be played in the stadium, where the grass is in much better shape than on our practice field.

Ibby and I are going to make signs so we can hang them around the school and get some fans out for the game. It always makes me feel bad when there are big crowds for the boys' football games, even though their record is 1 and 9, and hardly anyone fills the stands for girls' soccer, and we have a record of 12 and 1. Bo tried to console me when I mentioned this to him. "Don't worry, boys' soccer doesn't get a huge crowd, either, and most of the fans at the football games are parents watching their kids in the marching band."

Last warm-up ball drill is where you pair up with a partner and run backward while she tosses the ball at your head and you head it back to her. You do this for the entire width of the field and then trade spots and toss the ball at her head. I'm paired with Brittany, who gives the muddy ball a swipe on her soccer shorts.

"Don't bother," I say. "We're going to be covered with it before this practice is over!"

The whistle blows. I backpedal. Brit tosses. Arms out at my side for balance, I lean back, keeping my eye on the ball, and then quickly whip my upper body forward to meet the ball at my hairline. *Whump!*

"Back at you," I say.

Brit laughs out loud. "Tess, you should see yourself. Looks like someone threw a scoop of chocolate ice cream at your forehead!"

I wipe my face with my sleeves. "Laugh now, but it's your turn next!"

When we reach the sideline, I look over at the boys' field. Bo is totally covered in mud. He looks like a giant mud monster or a chocolate goalie from an Easter basket. I can tell by the flash of his white teeth every time he gets up from a save that he's loving every minute of it.

After we drill and play two-on-three, coach calls us in for a scrimmage. Eyeing us, she smiles. "I'm sorry, girls, but I can't help thinking that this practice couldn't have fallen on a better day. If you don't wash, you can frighten the entire town tomorrow night, trick-or-treating."

The boys' team runs over to us. Bo pulls Alex by his cleat in the mud, while Alex scoops up handfuls of muck and whips them at Bo's back.

"Wait a minute, boys!" Coach shouts, and they quiet down.

"Are we scrimmaging them today?" we ask.

"Hey, Munro. You look like a giant turd," shouts Bo.

I wipe my face with my muddy sleeve. "And you smell like one."

Not only do we love scrimmaging the boys, but somehow, now that we're all completely covered in mud, it feels like the ultimate equalizer. It reminds me of a word from an e. e. cummings poem we read in primary school—*mudluscious*.

Coach raises her hands for silence. "Yes, we're scrimmaging the boys. Now, settle down and listen up!"

"Tess, whenever you're not on offense, I want you to practice the game plan for #3 next week by marking Alex when he's on our half of the field. Understand?"

I study Alex—he's about my height and all muscle. He's the fastest player on the boys' team, with incredible ball skills.

A lot like Ramapo's blond warrior princess. My heart pounds
in my chest, but I place my hands on my hips and say, "Sure,
Coach."

"And fullbacks—hunt that ball down and clear it out to the
sides of the field. If you don't, they're going to kick it right back
down our throats! Do you hear me? Concentrate. No lapses. No
mistakes!"

Restless to begin, the defense nods their heads and stamps
designs in the mud with their cleats.

Coach turns to the boys' coach and says, "Mind if I have the
honors today?"

"They're all yours! I'll run the lines."

Center field, Coach has the whistle in her mouth, about to
signal the start of the scrimmage. With a mischievous grin, she
says, "Let's have a good, clean game today."

"Ha," I laugh. "Too late for that!"

The whistle blows.

We run, slide, slip, dive, kick, score, pick ourselves up, and
play our hearts out until it's time to go home. I tail Alex whenever I'm not on offense, and he doesn't score a single goal.
When the final whistle blows, we can barely see the soccer ball
in the fading light as we chase after it in our mud-covered
cleats.

⚽

"Muddy clothes off in the garage!" shouts a voice from inside.

For a minute, I worry that there's been a mother swap and
Ibby's mom and mine have traded places. I look down at my

practice clothes and realize that you can't even make out the original color of the T-shirt and shorts. Everything's stained a deep brown.

"Mom, she's a total pig," Mark says. He kicks off his sneakers in the hallway, snorts at me a few times, and slams the door in my face.

I'm going to kill my brother. When he picked me up from practice, he told me I had to ride in the trunk of the car because he didn't want to get the seats muddy. This from the slob who has a mountain of dirty laundry in the middle of his bedroom. Whenever he runs out of clean clothes, he picks from the heap and throws the stuff into his laundry bag, adds baby powder, shakes, and then wears it all over again.

Eventually, Mark agreed to let me sit in the backseat on some old maps from the glove compartment, but I had to promise to pay for replacements. Who knows, maybe he's planning a cross-country road trip, and I can look forward to some peace.

Sitting on the concrete step in front of the garage door leading to the house, I take off my socks. They look like they've been dipped in chocolate milk. I stuff some old newspapers from the recycling bin inside my cleats. Luke used to do this with his football shoes, said it helps absorb the dampness. Hopefully, they'll be dry for my last practice on Monday. Putting on wet cleats is as uncomfortable as trying to get into a wet bathing suit.

Inside, I smell Dad's homemade chili simmering on the stove. Corn muffins cool on the counter, and Mom is opening up a bag of prewashed salad.

Dad goes to give me a hug but has second thoughts. "Your mom told you to take those dirty clothes off in the garage!"

I try to grab a muffin, but he turns his back and boxes me out.

"My cleats are outside. I'm not walking around naked."

"No one'd notice," says Mark, with his mouth full of muffin.

"Dad, he got one!"

"He's clean. Put your clothes in the laundry room and take a shower in the downstairs bathroom, then we'll eat as a family."

I stomp into the laundry room to strip. *Eat as a family*— must be a full moon tonight, or Dr. Dad had a really bad case at school today, one where he noted in his report, *"Family rarely eats together."*

And stupid Mark! What does he mean, no one would notice? So I don't have a big chest like his stuck-up girlfriend across the street. Who needs all that bouncing when playing sports, anyway? Boobs just get in the way.

In the shower, I sing a song that Katie sang in the locker room at school:

Do your boobs hang low?
Do they wobble to and fro?
Can you tie 'em in a knot?
Can you tie 'em in a bow?
Can you throw 'em over your shoulder?
Will they grow bigger as you get older?
Do your boobs hang low?

I rinse the shampoo out of my hair and look down at my sudsy chest. Nope—couldn't even tie 'em in a knot. But my legs are lean, muscular, and strong—all I'm going to need next Tuesday to win that game against Ramapo.

Bam! Bam! on the bathroom door.

"Quit singing to your boobs, Tess, and get out here for dinner!" Mark shouts. "I'm starving and I'm going to be late!"

I wrap a towel around my hair and use another one for my body. I write on the steamy bathroom mirror, Mark is a big fat Dork! Below it, I draw a picture of his face looking cross-eyed and pimply.

Humming Katie's song, I smile at my reflection through the steam.

No wonder Mark's in a rush to eat tonight. He's got another date with Jillian. Her school's having a Halloween party, and she and Mark are going as Mark Antony and Cleopatra.

"Get it?" he says. "*Mark* Antony!"

"Get what?" I ask.

"Oh, that's right. You haven't studied Shakespeare, or much of anything, yet."

I hate it when he talks to me like I'm an idiot who doesn't know anything, just because he's in high school and, by some miracle or bribe, passed his driver's test, and I'm still in middle school. "I know the play *Julius Caesar*," I say. "Big deal, you're *Mark* Antony and Jillian's Cleopatra—Queen of *denial*."

Mark smirks and grabs one last muffin before getting up from the table. "It's Queen of the Nile, dope."

"It's *denial* if she's going out with you."

"Ha," he says snapping the back of my head with the wet dishtowel.

"Mom!"

Mom's trying very hard not to laugh. "Mark—where are you going in such a hurry, and what time will you be home?"

"Told Jillian I'd pick her up twenty minutes ago, and because of muddy Munro over here, with her half hour shower, I'm late." He makes another face at me behind their backs. "The dance is at St. Jude's. Be back by one or so."

"Midnight! Be careful driving, Mark. Don't rush."

But Mark has already grabbed a white sheet from the laundry room for his toga and is running out the door. No time for the Mom-and-Dad safety lecture.

I'm blowing on a hot spoonful of chili when I hear the crash. It sounds like metal hitting splintering wood. From the expressions on my parents' faces, I know their first thought is for Mark's safety, and their second, the new mailbox. But to my ears, the sound was much louder than a car hitting a mailbox.

It gives me hope.

We run to the front door. My father is always lecturing us to find the win–win solution to all our problems, and from my perspective, Mark scores tonight. He's standing outside his car and he appears to be okay—win. The mailbox is intact—win. However, the O'Hanlons' JUST VOTE NO sign is demolished!

In his rush to pick up Jillian, apparently Mark threw the car in reverse and kept right on going until he barreled into the offending sign with his rear bumper.

Everyone crowds around the scene of the collision. Mr. and Mrs. O'Hanlon; the two younger girls; Jillian, dressed in four-inch heels and a white satin toga that should have been rated triple X; the yappy poodles with their painted nails; my parents;

and Mark, looking embarrassed as he apologizes to the O'Hanlons and offers to duct-tape their sign back together.

I want to run up to Mark and hug him. Sure, I'm glad he's not hurt, but I'm also happy the obnoxious sign lies crushed under his back tires on the O'Hanlons' front lawn.

After all this, I can't believe that Jillian still wants to go to the Halloween dance with Mark. She has her priorities straight—appearances before politics. With Mom behind the wheel of her car, I watch as Jillian and Mark climb into the backseat—my parents wisely refuse to let Mark drive anywhere else tonight.

Satisfied, I stand on the sidewalk in front of our home and wave as they drive by.

From the backseat, Mark winks at me and gives me a thumbs-up.

I laugh out loud. I love that dorky brother of mine. I really do.

CHAPTER THIRTEEN

Early Saturday morning, I'm weeding the O'Hanlons' front lawn as part of my punishment for putting up the yard signs without their permission. It's not as bad as I thought it would be, because every time I look at the crushed JUST VOTE NO levy sign, I feel like laughing out loud.

After I finish, I head over to Bo's. He promised to help Ibby and me decorate for the haunted house tonight. It's our last chance before Election Day to get the word out and raise some money to pay for the campaign.

At first, there's no sign of the nosey bubble-headed bikers. I'm about to ring the Taubers' doorbell, when I spy them swinging from an old tire hanging from a huge elm.

"Hi!" I give them a friendly wave.

They stop practically midswing and stare. Little kids never forget.

"You gonna wake Bo up again?"

"Nope, this time I'm sure he's up, because he promised to help decorate for a haunted house we're having over at the Blooms' tonight. You kids should come. It's going to be *really* scary."

The runny-nose one turns to the other and says knowingly, "She's gonna wake Bo up."

I can't win. I ring Bo's doorbell once, twice, three times.

No answer.

They've abandoned the tire and are patiently standing on the property line, watching.

"He's probably in the shower," I call over my shoulder.

My fan club sits down in the grass. This could take a while.

"You better not be asleep, Bo!" I mutter.

I ring the doorbell in three quick bursts—nothing.

"Hey, you guys remember that fun game we played last time I was here?"

They nod—sure, they remember.

"Want to play again?"

Nope, they shake their heads. They'll sit this one out.

What happened to the eager little kids I remember being when I was their age? The ones who would risk playing in traffic if a teenager suggested that kissing hubcaps was the thing to do. "Why not?" I demand.

"Bo'd be mad," says the girl.

They're loyal all right, but their allegiance is to the five-foot-eleven, wise-mouthed goalie snoring his head off inside. For Bo's birthday next month, I'm getting him an alarm clock without a snooze button. I have an idea. "Hey, you kids want to practice for trick-or-treating tonight?"

That gets their attention.

"Practice?"

"Sure, when you get into . . . what grade are you in?"

"First."

"First grade—it's not guaranteed that you automatically get candy when you ring a doorbell. The competition is tough, and if you don't have your trick-or-treat method down, well, you might be out of luck. They'll save all the bad leftover candy from last year for you. Licorice jelly beans, old, hard caramels, sugar-free lollipops."

"Sugar-free?" they say. "Let's practice."

"First, we'll give Bo the trick. *You* go inside your house, call his phone number, and ask if his refrigerator's running. When he says yes, then you say, 'Then why don't you catch it?' And *you*, ring the front doorbell over and over again, while I tap and holler outside his window. When he comes to the door, we'll all shout *'Trick or Treat!'* Then he'll give us the *practice* candy."

When Bo finally appears at the door, he says, "Man, this is *baaad* déjà vu. From now on, don't sign me up for anything before twelve noon on Saturdays."

He doesn't even bother to tie a bandana around his head, just lets his dreads go wild.

"Do you have any candy in the house? I promised those two a practice treat if they helped."

"Bribed them? Pretty low, Tess. Anyway I ate all the candy. My mom says she's picking up some more for tonight on her way home from work. So they're flat out of luck."

"Come on, Bo. You've got to have some sort of candy."

"My grandma might have something. Let me check."

Bo comes out of the house with a plastic jar full of multi-colored disks and asks them which color they want.

"Those are Tums. Bo, you can't give them an antacid!"

"Why? You guys are giving me heartburn."

I take a Post-it note from my purse and write them an IOU for the candy and sign it. "Come to the haunted house tonight and we'll let you in for free," I promise. They seem to brighten a bit, but I have the feeling they would have been happier with the Tums.

When we get to Ibby's house, Bo whistles as we make our way up their circular driveway. "The Blooms went all out for this one."

And they did.

Painted plywood tombstones poke up from the ground with the names of teams the Cleveland Indians have recently defeated in the playoffs. Huge pumpkins line the walkway up to the front door. There are cobwebs all over the front porch, with fake black-widow spiders hanging from them.

Mixed in with all the Halloween decorations are signs supporting the school levy. A ghost's says, *Vote Yes for our schools: a boo-tiful place to learn!* A witch stirs a bubbling cauldron that reads, *Cast a yes vote for our schools!*

"It looks like they're all ready for tonight."

Ibby opens the door. "Where have you guys been? I've been waiting for over an hour."

I give Bo a look. "I had to weed the O'Hanlons' lawn, and Bo wouldn't answer his door again this morning."

Ibby walks us outside and around back to the garage. She punches in a code and the doors open.

"*Hellooo* pumpkins!" says Bo.

"Oh my God, Ibs—where did you get so many pumpkins?"

"Did my mom go overboard?"

"She raided a freaking pumpkin patch," says Bo.

"What are we going to do with so many?"

Ibby hands me a special carving knife, serrated on both sides. "Carve?"

I try to count the hundreds of different-size pumpkins that are sitting on top of tables and workbenches, piled in baskets, surrounding golf bags, bicycles, and gardening tools. There's even one forty-pounder resting on the seat of a riding lawn mower. "Ibs, we could carve for the entire day and not even half of these would be jack-o'-lanterns by the time the haunted house opens tonight!"

"Imagine how cool it would be to have all these glowing pumpkin faces lining the driveway?"

Bo grabs a carving knife. "Come on, Munro. Get to work." And with that, he cuts out a little circular stem cap from the top of the nearest pumpkin.

Ibby lays down newspapers and Bo reaches inside the pumpkin with both hands and scoops out the seeds. "Pumpkin guts!" he says, and throws the tangled wet mass onto the nearest papers.

Splat.

I don't know if it's the smell of pumpkin goo or the stringy, seedy glob quivering on the garage floor, but all of a sudden, I get the dry heaves and feel like I'm going to lose my breakfast.

Bo laughs. "Tess Munro—big, tough soccer player can't handle a little pumpkin puke!"

Ibby smiles as she carves a toothy grin on her pumpkin.

"Stop it, Bo!" I gag. "I've never"—gag—"liked . . . scooping"—cough-gag—

I run over to the other side of the car so they can't see me if I throw up. Once I'm away from the pumpkin smell, I feel better.

"Hey, Munro, better not hurl on those Beamer hubcaps."

"Shut up, Tauber!"

Feeling a little light-headed, I sit down on the driveway and lean my head against the car door. "I like jack-o'-lanterns," I try to explain. "It's just something about the smell of pumpkin guts."

"Aw, you'll get used to it."

Ibby comes around the side of the car with a couple of shopping bags. "You okay, Tess? You can work on these."

Inside the bags are the bitty baby pumpkins—no bigger than my hand.

"You won't have to cut a thing, just paint the outsides, okay?"

I nod, grateful to have a job that doesn't involve the loss of my dignity or the doughnuts I inhaled for breakfast this morning.

It turns out that Bo has a gift for pumpkin carving. He makes some look like black cats, bats, ghosts, and vampires, but the most amazing ones resemble teachers at our school.

There's a squat, round Mr. Ramella with Elvis Presley hair, and a pumpkin with Ms. Harper's straight, China-doll haircut. But the best is Mrs. Bustamonte. For that creation, Bo carved out her small wire-rim glasses and short, spiky do. Best of all is the mousetrap he found in Ibby's garage and attached to the dried pumpkin vine on top of her head.

"Bo! You can't do that," Ibby says. "What if she's here tonight and sees it?"

"People never see themselves as they really are. And if she even shows, I bet she won't notice it."

"She notices everything!" I say.

"Then why can't she catch the kid who's stealing mouse balls?"

"Maybe it's not a kid who's taking them. Maybe it's a custodian or a substitute teacher or Vice Principal Korn sneaking into the Tech lab at night," I offer.

"Why would the vice principal or a janitor steal the mouse balls?" Bo asks.

I shrug. "To sell on eBay?"

Bo turns to Ibby. "Is that nontoxic paint Munro's inhaling over there?"

Ibby makes a face and continues carving, traditional jack-o'-lanterns with varying-size triangles and toothless grins. "I think Sarah said she found most of the mouse balls along the wall in the gym."

"Aha!" I say. "Wadler's the culprit."

"No," says Bo. "It just means that when kids steal 'em, they think they're getting some sort of high-bouncing Superball, but mouse balls don't bounce. They just kinda go *blunk*."

Ibby and I ask the logical next question. "How would you know?"

"Um . . . I just do," Bo says with a sheepish smile.

"Klepto!" I go back to painting my tenth baby-pumpkin face. Only this one has a big O for a mouth. "Hey, look, guys." I come out from behind the car and line up ten little pumpkins in a row. I incorporated one letter on each pumpkin face to spell out *S-a-v-e S-p-o-r-t-s*.

"Great idea, Tess," says Ibs.

"Thanks. Think it'll help?"

Bo stops carving a pumpkin that looks suspiciously like our librarian in her Dutch-girl costume. For once, he appears to seriously consider my question.

"It'll be close. But I think people will go for it. Why wouldn't they want us to have sports and stuff?"

Bo grabs a soccer ball–sized pumpkin and hugs it to his chest, shouting, "Don't separate a goalie from his ball, man! It's too cruel!"

"I guess I'd miss swimming, too," says Ibs. "Definitely wouldn't want to see Ms. Harper or Mr. Chen lose their jobs."

"Definitely miss taking the bus if my brother has to drive me to school every day," I mumble.

Ibby looks alarmed. "I'd walk, Tess."

"Or run," says Bo. "Next to the car!"

"Very funny." I make a face at Bo. But suddenly it's not. Not funny at all, and I feel that queasy sick feeling again in my stomach as I look around at all the pumpkins and think about what's at stake.

"We've got to win," I say. "We've just got to."

CHAPTER FOURTEEN

A Halloween costume says a lot about a person. We're not little kids anymore, with our parents dressing us in store-bought costumes that reveal their hopes and expectations as we run around the neighborhood as little doctors, pro-athletes, and brides. I feel sorry for my mom. She never got off easy. When Luke was younger, he was into natural disasters and insisted on being a tornado for Halloween. Then he got into space and astronomy, and Mom went to work on a solar system costume, complete with orbiting Styrofoam planets.

It was a relief by the time I was old enough to request a costume, because I was happy to wear Mark's and Luke's hand-me-down sports uniforms for Halloween. A football, baseball, soccer player—it didn't matter to me as long as I got to carry a candy bag and a ball.

Which is why it doesn't surprise me that Olivia Fletcher ditched the angel costume she wore the other day at school and tonight, struts around in a red satin devil's outfit, carrying a pitchfork and bossing everyone around. Even Ibby's cat, Cheshire, scurries out of Olivia's way.

Ibby, Bo, and I did most of the planning and work for tonight, but it's Olivia who positions herself at the front door to collect the three-dollar admission fee and acts like having the haunted house was all her idea and effort. I feel like borrowing her pitchfork and butting her out of the way but decide that ignoring her is probably the best policy.

I walk around taking in the transformation. I have to hand it to the Blooms because the Halloween decorations fit their castle-like home perfectly. The pictures on the wall hang crooked and upside down, with silky cobwebs trailing everywhere. The lights are dim and spooky music plays in the background. A black carpet winds its way through the living room, dining room, and downstairs into the basement, where the Frankenstein beanbag toss, a toilet paper mummy wrap, and Guess the Gruesome Goo are set up around the room.

Ibby mans the goo station, where she has a bowl of spaghetti, which she insists is intestines, grapes for eyeballs, and a wobbly Jell-O–mold brain. She informs visitors that they're on their way to a transplant operation being performed at midnight at a witches' warren.

By ten p.m., it feels like the entire school is here. Mrs. Bloom seems to be holding up pretty well. The only thing that gives away her anxiety is the voice pitched five octaves above normal and the fact that she's wringing her hands, probably wishing that we'd all turn into pumpkins at the stroke of midnight and roll out of sight.

We don't make it to midnight.

Around ten thirty, I'm wandering around, looking for Ibby's missing cat, calling, "Chesie, Chesie, Chesie." Ibby named Cheshire after the vanishing cat in *Alice in Wonderland*, and Chesie's wasted no time disappearing tonight, with the doors opening and closing every time a parent drops off a trick-or-treater.

Peering under an old pine tree in the backyard, I'm think-ing that if losing Chesie for a few hours is the worst thing that happens tonight, we made out pretty good, when suddenly, all hell breaks loose. I race toward the sounds of crashing furni-ture and screaming coming from the basement, where Bo and Joey Montanado are trying to wrestle each other to the floor.

"What happened?" I shout to Katie, who tries to hop out of the way as the boys stumble, tumble, and twist up the stairs and out onto the Blooms' back patio.

"Joey threw the intestines at Bo, and then Bo grabbed the brain—watch out, Tess!"

I leap out of the way as they come crashing back toward us.

As Joey and Bo roll off the patio and into the flowerbeds, I'm afraid they might smash one of Mrs. Bloom's garden gnomes. I make a grab for Bo, but it's difficult to get at him in his mammo box, which is crushed and mangled from the fight.

Besides, my own costume doesn't afford much mobility— a homemade outfit that I threw together at the last minute, fashioned entirely of duct tape—a tribute to my dad, who uses it as an all-purpose fix-it around our home. And not too shabby if I do say so myself. Maybe if I took an inch or so off the sleeves, I could duct-tape Joey and Bo's arms to their sides and end this thing. And while I'm at it, I'll tape their trashy mouths shut, too. If Mrs. Bloom hears this language, she'll enroll Ibs in a private girls' school tomorrow.

Any minute now, I expect her to appear in her Queen Eliz-abeth costume and shout, "Off with their heads!"

"Bo!" I shout. "Cut it out, you're going to break something!"

I guess when you're busy trying to beat the crap out of someone, you're not about to take orders from duct-tape girl.

Joey tries desperately to land some wild punches. He hits nothing but cardboard.

There's definitely more to this than Jell-O brains and spaghetti intestines. I bet it has to do with Bo offering Olivia a free mammogram earlier this evening if she'd stick her you-know-whats in the holes of his costume. Joey and Olivia have been on-again-off-again going out since sixth grade.

Lucky for the cardboard box. Although it restricts Bo's arms somewhat, it offers him protection against Joey's punches.

In the midst of all this commotion, I spy Cheshire darting across the back lawn and into the basement, carrying something in her mouth. One problem solved. Now, how do I get these two to break it up?

"They're trashing the backyard," Katie yells.

At the side of the house, there's a garden hose coiled over a wrought-iron hook. I dash for the faucet and turn it on full force. Grabbing the spray nozzle, I set it on jet stream. Ready, aim—*fire!*

A blast of cold water hits Bo and Joey. They fall back, stunned and soaking, to separate corners of the garden just as Ibby runs up the basement steps and onto the stone patio. "Oh, *nooo!*" she cries.

The garden beds are trampled and a gnome lies in pieces on the patio.

"Sorry, Ibs," pants Bo, standing there in his soggy box and spaghetti-smeared hair. He picks up a fragment of pottery from the gnome's red hat. "I'll try to glue it back together or buy your mom a new one. It's just that that stupid a—"

But Joey's nowhere in sight.

"He ran around front," says Katie.

"It's okay," says Ibby. "But we better hide it until it's fixed."

We help gather up the pieces and stick them underneath a leafy hydrangea that's dried on the stalk. "Did you find Cheshire?" she asks.

"I saw her during the fight. She ran back inside the house."

"Good." Ibby sighs with relief. "I was worried we'd never find her."

I hesitate. "Um . . . Cheshire had something in her mouth."

Ibby looks horrified, but I'm not surprised. Every time I see my neighbor's cat, Spooks, he's hunting chipmunks or birds, and once, he even tangled with a baby skunk, which earned him a tomato-juice bath.

"A mouse?" asks Ibby.

"Bigger."

Ibby groans. "My mother's going to freak! Oh, Tess, this is so not turning out the way I imagined—the basement is trashed, Mr. Brownie's head is crushed—"

"Mr. Brownie?"

"My mother names the gnomes." She looks around, surveying the flowerbeds, and sighs, "And most of the plants are destroyed."

I pat her back. "Sorry, Ibs. Don't worry about the mess. Bo and I will get the soccer teams to help—"

Katie comes racing around the corner and practically crashes into us as she slips on the wet grass.

"You better come quick, you guys! Bo and Joey are at it again, only this time, they're smashing pumpkins in the street!"

Poor Ibs looks so frightened. This night is spinning out of control. Like Metz always says, "Objects in motion stay in motion."

Ibby and I run to the street and can't believe the scene in front of us. If carving pumpkins gave me the dry heaves earlier today, then surely this disgusting mess is enough to make any-one puke.

Bo, Joey, Brittany, and some other kids are in the middle of the street in front of the Blooms' house. The fluorescent street-lights hum and cast a ghoulish glow on everyone as they grab pumpkins from the front lawn and smash them on the asphalt road.

Laughing and screaming, everyone slips and slides on pumpkin guts.

Bo runs and then belly flops headfirst, his costume a slimy mess, as he skids the length of the street, stopping only when he hits the sewer grate next to the curb.

Without saying a single word, Ibby turns and walks back toward the house.

I'm torn. The good-friend part of me wants to follow Ibby and tell her everything's going to be all right. But the loves-mud-soccer part wants to join in the pumpkin bash. I grab a small pumpkin from the front lawn and roll it at Bo like it's a bowling ball. "Knock it off, Bo!" I shout. It hits him in the foot and he falls. Strike!

Laughing, he vows revenge.

Brittany, dressed as a Goth chick, beats him to it when she throws some pumpkin guts at my face. I feel the large white seeds sticking to my cheeks. I smell pumpkin innards again and feel my stomach begin to churn. Wiping the sticky seeds away with the back of my hand, I consider my choices—puke or play?

Just then, Alex slides by my feet, using the lid of one of the Blooms' garbage cans. "Yippeeeeeyah!" he shouts.

Definitely *play*. I don't want to miss out on the fun!

Smash! Smash! Smash! Pumpkins hit the pavement, exploding their gooey mess everywhere. Olivia comes running out to the street and screeches from the sidewalk, "You pigs are ruining the party!"

Katie nails her on the side of the head with some pumpkin shmam and Olivia retreats back into the house waving her pitchfork, her pointy devil's tail twitching behind her.

My duct tape costume, combined with the pumpkin filling, offers excellent sliding opportunity. Reminds me of another one of Metz's lessons on friction, but I can't think of the scientific law right now, with all the chaos and commotion around me.

I catch a glimpse of Bo's bubble-headed bikers standing on the sidewalk, open-mouthed and staring. They've come to collect on the candy I owe them. The runny-nosed one points me out in the crowd. I don't need to be a lip reader to understand what he's saying. "Bet you this is all her fault!"

My fault? I look around at the destruction. The street looks like it's coated with pumpkin pie filling. Ibby's parents are going to kill her. What about all the beautifully carved pumpkins? What about my *Save Sports* pumpkins?

Dressed as Noah, Georgie Taxus stands on the sidewalk holding them in his arms as if he were saving the baby gourds from an apocalyptic flood—exactly what we're going to need to wash this mess away. "So you wanna *save sports?*" he cries. Smash-bash-crash! The bitty pumpkins hit the street and shatter into a hundred pulpy pieces.

Georgie looks so pleased with himself that I laugh out loud—until I spy Ibby scurrying down the driveway, carrying a shield in front of her.

"Oh, no!" I cry.

Ibs looks like a fierce lioness stalking her prey. What is she doing? I check out the craziness all around and wish that there were some way I could protect her.

She hesitates at the sidewalk with the saucer-sled raised high and blue plastic grocery bags covering the paws of her lion costume.

Bo sees her and stops mashing stringy pumpkin guts into Alex's punk spiked hair.

Katie asks, "What's up with the bags, Ibs?"

Ibby looks at all of us with a determined expression on her face and shouts, "Happy Halloween!" and launches herself into the middle of the road on her shield. She slides for a good twenty feet before she comes to rest just around the cul-de-sac bend.

Everyone whoops and hollers, "Way to go, Ibby!"

I slip and stumble toward her and finally crawl the last couple of yards on my hands and knees. I'm laughing so hard, I think I pee in my pants. When I reach Ibby, I wrap my slimy duct-tape arms around her and give her the biggest hug.

And even after the police officers show up and one asks, "Haven't we met before, Miss Munro?" and we stand sorry and subdued in front of Mrs. Bloom, and Cheshire strolls in and drops a present of a live mole on the white carpet at her feet, and I promise to spend the entire next day and every day cleaning up the mess from our first *and last* Halloween bash and to replace the gnome and replant the flowers and rethink my actions and readjust my attitude. . . . I know without a doubt that it was all worth it!

CHAPTER FIFTEEN

Monday morning at school, everyone is talking about the amazing Halloween party at Ibby's house. Mark even said that some of his high school buddies were buzzing about this middle school bash where they smashed pumpkins and went sledding on the guts. "Way to go, Tess," he says. "None of that kiddie shaving-creamed cars or toilet-papering houses for you!"

Praise from Mark is rare, so I don't tell him that it was Bo and Joey's fight that started it all.

Juvenile delinquency has its price. Sitting in Science class, my neck and lower back hurt from the all-day cleanup at the Blooms' on Sunday. It's impossible to find a comfortable position. The others don't look in any better shape.

Ibby's taking notes with her head resting on her arm, and Bo looks like a pile of laundry thrown in the corner, with his body slumped over the desk and his hoodie pulled up over his head. They're hurting, too. It's easy smashing and sledding on pumpkins. It's a lot harder hosing down and scrubbing the entire street and picking up pumpkin pieces—enough to fill twelve heavy-duty trash bags.

Poor Mrs. Bloom. She had been doing so well that night, too, at least up until the shrieks and shouting brought her out to the street. She lost it right there at the end of her driveway, when she saw her daughter covered in orange slime, slipping and sliding across the road.

Ibby says her mom's been talking about living in a bios-phere and the benefits of homeschooling.

Ibby has no regrets. With one wild party, she ditched her geekess image and has shot right to the top of our class as dar-ing, creative, and cool. Something I've always known about her anyway.

From my window seat, I look out over the soccer fields and feel really sad that our last practice is this afternoon. A flock of Canada geese grazes on the field, depositing green turds wher-ever they walk. I daydream, imagining them challenging the seagulls to a soccer game and kicking a goal with their wide webbed feet or heading the ball into the net with their beaks. Or would that be a beak ball? Canada Geese 1–Seagulls 0!

"So what do you think . . . Tess?"

Busted!

"Sorry, Mr. Metz, I wasn't—"

"Paying attention? You're not on that field yet," he says with a smile.

How can he smile? Calypso is history after the biting inci-dent with Georgie, and rumor has it that Metz is being forced to give equal time to intelligent design.

I slump down in my chair and rest my chin on my knuck-les. I have a feeling that whether the levy passes or not, Mr. Metz won't stick around Clarkstown Middle School teaching science for much longer.

At the thought of the election tomorrow, my stomach makes a growling noise like I'm hungry, only I'm not because I just had lunch, and my mechanical pencil feels slippery between my fingers. Our school's closed tomorrow because they can't control security with voters coming in and out of the building all day. Since we won't be in classes, Olivia's called a final levy meeting after school to organize which polling places we'll stand in front of with our signs tomorrow.

I painted a sign of my own the other night, with a huge S.O.S. on it, in our school colors, orange and black. Underneath, I wrote, *Save Our Sports!*

"Nice, Tess," Mark said. "Got to hand it to you. You definitely have a one-track mind."

He's wrong.

I have a two-track mind—winning our last soccer game of the season and helping the school levy pass!

⚽

Olivia stands in front of the chalkboard with her flip chart of polling locations and the names of the volunteers assigned to each. She distributes stickers she'd like us to wear on our clothes and posters we're to display so people can see them as they walk into the churches, synagogues, and schools to cast their vote.

"I've made my own sign," I say when she goes to hand me one.

"Can't use your own sign," Olivia says. "It's not officially approved."

"Approved by who?" I ask.

"By me!"

"Who made you the levy queen?" I look to Ms. Harper for help on this one, but she quickly looks the other way, evidently following my father's philosophy of letting the kids work it out for themselves.

"I'm the *president* of this committee," Olivia says in a snarky voice, "and I have final approval on *all* signs."

I bet this has more to do with pumpkin pulp pelting Olivia's big head the other night than with sign approval.

"Whatever," I say, not wanting to get into an argument and miss even more soccer practice than I already have. I head for the door. "I'll show you the sign tomorrow and you can approve it or not, but now, I'm going to practice."

"Not yet!" She frantically flips through her charts. "I haven't told you where you're posted for Election Day."

Right now, the only place I want to be posted is next to the goalpost, waiting for that corner kick to come flying over the defenders' heads so I can one-time it into the back of the net!

The flip chart falls off its metal stand and lands in a crumpled mess on the floor. Olivia fusses and kneels down to retrieve it.

Bo was so right to ditch this last meeting. What a waste of time! Outside Ms. Harper's window, I see my team has finished warm-ups and is hard at work drilling for tomorrow's game.

"I've got to go, Olivia!" Is she doing this on purpose? I wonder.

"Okay, okay . . . here it is!" She reads, "Tess Munro and Bo Tauber—St. Jude's Catholic High School from twelve noon until two p.m."

"Got it—bye!" I race down the hallway. The *clickity-clack* of my cleats echoes off the tile floor. Free at last! It's not until I'm on the field running my seven laps for being late that it hits me. *St. Jude's?* Oh, great, I'm forced to stand in front of Jillian O'Hanlon's high school.

I pick up the pace, practically sprinting the last lap. Maybe I should stand in front of her school dressed in my soccer uniform for my game later that afternoon and have my shin guards on for protection. Who am I kidding? The abuse won't be physical. And plastic shin guards are no match against an army of Jillians.

⚽

After practice, I struggle with my laundry, which is piled up in my room, along with the muddy practice clothes I left fermenting like a forgotten science experiment in the laundry tub. Okay, I admit that I'm not much better than Mark is when it comes to keeping up with the wash. I don't pay attention when sorting the colors and whites. And sometimes I forget to check the pockets and wind up with bubble gum stuck to my jeans after I pull them out of the dryer, money going through the wash, and the biggest disaster—the green gel pen that exploded all over my bras and underpants. Tie-dye anyone?

Eww! The muddy practice shorts and T-shirt from last week smell like the time my dad went grocery shopping in the summer and forgot the eggs in the trunk for a week. I grab the bottle of bleach to get rid of this stench so I can wear these practice clothes for basketball this winter—*if* we have basketball this winter!

As the washing machine fills, I spy the new bleach pen my mother put on the shelf for spot stains.

"Tess, goalie boy's on the phone!"

I'm going to kill my brother. I grab my jeans from the dirty laundry pile and sit on the dryer cradling the phone between my ear and shoulder.

"Hey, Tess, so where did Queen Olivia station us for tomorrow's blitzkrieg?"

"St. Jude's—twelve to two."

"Hmm, that's doable."

"Bo, if you're not awake and ready to go by eleven thirty, I swear I'll—"

"Tess-ty! Tess-ty! Don't worry. I'll be ready. Just stop by and pick me up, okay? It's only about two blocks from my house."

"Don't oversleep. I've traumatized those two little neighbors of yours enough. If they see me pounding on your door again, they'll call the cops. Officer Todd and I are on a first-name basis. He told my mom that the pumpkin bash was strike two. One more and—"

"Bye, Tess. Got a ton of homework. I'm hanging up now . . ."

"Yeah, sure, you don't have a record like I—"

"Hanging up the phone . . . now!"

"Bo, wait!"

"What?"

"Think we'll win, tomorrow?"

Silence.

"Bo?"

"Yeah?"

"Think the school levy's going to pass?"

"Hey, Tess," he says in a quiet, serious voice, one I so rarely hear from Bo Tauber's mouth that I press the phone against my ear in order to catch every word.

"Don't worry about it, okay? The only passing you should be thinking about is the passing that comes in front of the goal at your game tomorrow."

I hang up the phone smiling. Bo's right. Scoring a couple of goals during tomorrow's game is something I have control over. Everything else is out of my hands now.

CHAPTER SIXTEEN

When I wake up this morning, the first thing on my mind is Election Day. Why can't I be eighteen so I can vote? At thirteen, all I can do is beg other people for theirs. Still, I'm hopeful that we'll win both the levy and the game before the day is over.

When I pull the clothes from the wash that I ran last night, I inspect my jeans. *"Yesss!"* I say out loud.

Mark pauses at the laundry-room door and asks, "What did you do to your jeans?"

"Wrote *S.O.S.*—which stands for *Save Our Sports* all over them with the bleach pen. Cool, huh?"

Mark shrugs and takes a bite of his toaster waffle. "I guess. You've got a future as a graffiti artist."

"I'm going to wear them today when I stand in front of St. Jude's for the levy."

Mark grunts and begins to walk away. A second later, he pops his head back in the door. "St. Jude's?"

"Mmm-hmm." I throw my wet laundry into the dryer. "From twelve to two."

"Not in those jeans."

"Yeah, in these jeans."

"You'll look like a dork!"

"At least my clothes are clean. Hey, what's the matter? Afraid Jillian won't like 'em?"

"Nooo, I just don't want *my* little sister walking around like she's a mental moron."

"It's a great idea. A brilliant idea! And do I need to remind you, Mr. GQ, that *your* girlfriend wears ugly plaid and polyester to school every day?"

"You're really hung up on this sports thing passing, aren't you?"

I nod, feeling my throat tighten. I don't even try to say another word.

"Wear the jeans," Mark sighs. "If you like 'em, I guess that's all that matters."

⚽

I do like them. I admire them so much as I'm walking over to Bo's that I almost trip on the uneven sidewalks. Before I left the house, I took an even more creative approach and used different-color gel pens to write *Vote Yes* inside and around the bleached *S.O.S.* spots. I'm so excited to show Bo my Election Day creation that I walk right by the bobble-head twins sitting on their front steps.

"Hey, girl!" they call and run down to the sidewalk.

"Hi, guys. Do you like my jeans?" I ask, proudly extending my leg in front of them so they can get a closer look.

They try to sound out the word: "Vho ... tt ... eh ... y-yehs."

"Vote yes!" I help them. "Today's Election Day"—I show them my homemade levy sign—"people are going to the polls to vote for the school levy." I might as well say that people are flying to the moon for a milkshake for all they understand about polls and levies.

"Did you do that to your pants on purpose?" the girl asks.

"Yep!"

"Hmm," the boy says, walking around to get a view of the back side. "Hey, look," he points. "She even wrote on her butt!"

They crack up laughing.

"All right, that's enough." I shoo him away. They're obviously too little to appreciate walking art. As I head over to Bo's, I overhear them say, "That girl does a lot of bad things."

"Yeah," the other agrees. "When she grows up, they'll put her in jail."

I'm in the middle of pounding on Bo's door when, miraculously, it opens, and he's standing there completely dressed and ready to go, wearing a smug grin.

"Got ya!" he says, snapping his fingers in my face.

"I was just about to grab a rock from your grandma's garden and toss it at your window."

"I've been up for hours," he says, reaching behind his head to tie his dreads back. "Finished Harper's math packet and got a start on that project that's due on Friday for Metz."

I groan. "Don't remind me. I haven't even looked at it yet. Maybe tonight after the game." Yeah, right! I'll be too busy watching television for the levy results.

"St. Jude's?" he asks.

I nod. "You didn't notice my pants."

"*Hellooo,* pants!" Bo whistles. "But Tess, don't you think you're taking this—"

"Too far? Too serious? Too—?"

"Yeah, all of the above. How are you going to feel in a week or a month from now, walking around wearing *vote yes* on your butt?"

"I'll feel great, because it'll remind me of the day we won! Besides, if it changes even one person's mind at the polls, then it'll be worth it."

We arrive at St. Jude's in time to relieve Olivia from her post outside the front doors of the building where people are going in to vote. She glares at my homemade *Save Our Sports* sign.

"I thought I told you that you needed approval for that."

I hold the sign up in her face and say, "Olivia, may I?"

She squints her eyes and studies it for a minute. "Yes, you may. But next time, follow the rules."

"Hopefully, there won't be any next time," I say.

"Hey, Liv." Bo points to my jeans. "Does she need approval for those, too?"

Hands on hips, Inspector Olivia takes her job as president of the Clarkstown Middle School Student Levy Committee *waaay* too seriously when she says, "Technically, yes. After all, they are an advertisement for the levy."

"They don't say *school levy* on them. Just *S.O.S* and *vote yes*," I remind her. "Totally generic."

"But you're a public school student holding a school levy sign, and so by process of association—"

"You heard her, Tess. Off with your pants—right now!"

"Shut up, Bo." I cover my mouth with my sign, trying not to laugh.

"What's the matter?" he says. "Bleach your underwear, too?"

I try to hit him with my sign, but he ducks out of the way.

"I'm so out of here!" Olivia says. "Will you two try to stay out of trouble? And remember what Ms. Harper said—'play nice with the community!'"

Bo begins to jump around like a lunatic, growling and beating his chest with his fists. He sings out, "We're the mighty lions. The mighty, mighty lions! *Roooar!*"

He caps the performance with one of his trademark booming farts, with the intended effect of driving Olivia far away.

"You're such a pig, Bo Tauber!" Olivia calls over her shoulder as she beats a hasty retreat.

"What about you?" Bo says as he playfully hangs his arm over my shoulders and snorts in my ear. "You think I'm a pig?"

"No—just crazy."

An elderly couple, dressed like they're going to church, make their way up St. Jude's front walkway, heading for the doors where the miniature American flags are popping out of the ground. They eye us suspiciously.

I push Bo away and hold up my sign. "Please vote yes for the Clarkstown school levy!" I say, wearing what I hope is a winning smile.

The woman barely nods and refuses to make eye contact. The man gives Bo a stern look and holds open the door for Sourpuss as they make their way inside.

"Think they're a yes or a no?" asks Bo.

I kick at a pebble on the walkway. "Probably no," I sigh.

"How can you tell?"

"They wouldn't look us in the eye. Just like in *To Kill a Mockingbird,* the lawyer, Atticus, told his children that the jury never looks the defendant in the eye if they're voting against him."

"We're not on trial here, Tess."

"Maybe *we're* not," I mumble, "but our school is."

"Well, look who's here!" A familiar squeal pierces the glum silence.

"Bo Tauber! What are you doing hanging around an all-girls school? Looking for a date?" asks Jillian O'Hanlon.

Jillian's friends cackle at her lame joke.

Bo smiles. "Nope—just doing my part for my school, my team, and my country."

"Ha, ha, ha!" They sound like a bad laugh track from an old '80s sitcom.

"Give me a break," I mutter.

Suddenly, the Jillians stare at me like I'm a fresh rat turd newly deposited at their blessed front doorstep. Could it be the jeans?

Jillian turns to her clones, all identically dressed in navy-and-green plaid skirts with white blouses. "This is Mark's little sister."

"Tess Munro," I say.

They eye me from head to toe, taking an extra-long time on the jeans. One girl tilts her head and moves her lips as she reads my levy slogans. I don't need to be a mind reader to figure out that I'm not measuring up.

"Ahh, interesting jeans, Tess," says Jillian with a smirk.

Should I remind her that she walked around with the word *Dance* scrawled across her butt the entire summer? And what's the matter with a little team spirit for a good cause? Suddenly, I feel my arms sinking to my sides, weary from holding up my sign to flatline faces that hold the power over whether I'll be dribbling the ball on the court this winter or ever again.

Tough crowd.

But after all, we're stationed at a Catholic school. I'm sure that kids standing outside the public schools, American Legion Halls, and libraries are receiving a warm welcome—*Yay! Higher taxes. I'll vote for that!*

"Well, good luck!" Jillian chirps, all fake and phony. Everyone knows she had a billboard on her front lawn telling everyone to VOTE NO! And if it weren't for my brother's inability to master the concept of reverse, it'd still be standing today.

Jillian walks away with her friends and calls over her shoulder, "See you later, Tess!"

Is she planning another gymnastics exhibition on her front lawn? No—it's getting too cold for that now. Maybe she and Mark are going out tonight, but that wouldn't usually happen on a Tuesday. Jillian doesn't leave me in suspense for long.

"At your soccer game this afternoon."

"My soccer game?" I look at Bo for confirmation.

He shrugs. "That's what she said."

"Why would she come to my soccer game?"

"Anyone can attend. They're not invitation only. Vote yes!" Bo calls after a mom and two toddlers entering the doors. This time, the voter makes eye contact and smiles.

"Who'd invite her? Unless—I'm going to kill him!"

"Mark?"

"Who else!" I whip my S.O.S. sign around in frustration. "He never comes to any of my games. Why would he wait until the last one of the year to show his face? And if the action on the field's not enough to hold his attention-deficient brain for even sixty minutes, he has Jilly Bean there for entertainment."

"Jilly Bean?"

"That's what he calls her. Wonder if she plans on putting on a halftime show?"

"Forget it, Tess. What do you care if Jillian's there or not? You've got plenty of other things to think about if you're going to win today."

A businessman dressed in a crisp gray suit walks between us. "Excuse me," he says.

"Vote yes!" I halfheartedly wave my sign in his direction.

He grunts noncommittally.

"Do you think we'll win, Bo?"

"You've asked me that a hundred times! If I could read the future, I'd win all the Friday-night poker games."

"I just can't stand the suspense any longer! I feel like I've been in limbo for the past month. I want so badly to beat Ramapo and win this stupid levy."

"I think you've got a good chance—with both, Tess. Here—" He takes out a pen from his back pocket and kneels down— "I want to write something on your jeans."

"Hey, watch it!" I slap his hand away.

He makes a face. "Come on, I'm writing it on your leg."

I feel the pen's pressure. "What does it say? I can't read it from here."

He finishes and stands up. "You'll see it later. Now, let's grab something to eat before the game."

As we leave our posts outside St. Jude's, we run into Mrs. Bustamonte heading in to vote.

I wave and call to her, "Vote *yes*, Mrs. B.! Vote *yes!*"

She smiles and says, "Of course! And congratulations to the both of you on all your hard work."

"Thanks," we answer.

She adjusts her glasses and points to my pants. "Creative campaigning, Miss Munro!"

CHAPTER SEVENTEEN

After I take off my jeans to change for my game, I turn them over so I can read Bo's message. In blue ballpoint pen it says:

> Tess, it's not whether you win or lose but how you play the game — Bo

How have I played the game?

I remember all those meetings, knocking on people's doors for yard signs, raising $238 at the haunted house, and standing outside St. Jude's today and hopefully reminding voters what's at stake if it doesn't pass.

I pull on my shorts and socks. And in soccer, I've worked very hard both individually and with my team. I've taken on greater responsibilities for today's game in marking #3. I guess I've played the game as best as I can, but still, I can't resist writing a quote of my own beneath Bo's—one I remember Luke had taped on his bedroom wall, from a famous football coach he admired.

"Winning isn't everything. It's the only thing." —*Vince Lombardi*

And that's exactly how I plan on returning home here tonight—a winner!

⚽

I have a rule that when we're the home team, I try not to watch as the other team gets off the bus. I force myself to ignore them. I don't want to be intimidated. I try to stay focused on my warm-ups.

Today, I break this rule.

I measure and compare, trying to find a real or imaginary advantage for our team over theirs. Yet it's not like they're an unknown. We've played Ramapo before—and lost. It's going to be another tough game, even if in my completely unbiased pregame judgment, we appear to have the taller, stronger, more highly skilled players.

Of course there's always #3. She could tip the balance in their favor if she has another great game. Today, her long hair is braided in tiny rows, with red-and-white ribbon, her school colors, tying it all back in a ponytail. All her teammates wear matching ribbons.

Good—I hope they care more about fashion than foot skills!

"Tess, get your head in the game!" Coach calls, after watching me flub my second volley kick in a row.

"I will!"

"Nervous?" Katie asks.

"A little." I wipe the sweat off my forehead with my sleeve. "I've got that fluttery butterfly feeling in my stomach, and I feel like I need to pee one more time, even though the last time I tried, nothing came out."

"Don't worry, Tess. They don't look that tough." Katie tosses the ball at my thigh for our warm-up drill. "And someone's mom sure went a little overboard with the hair accessories."

I laugh. "Got that right!" I volley-kick it back to her hard, and point up into the stands. "Ibby's coming to watch the game today. My whole family's supposed to be here, too, including Mark and his stupid girlfriend."

"Wow, Mark has a girlfriend?"

"Jillian O'Hanlon. She called me a beast."

"You are a beast!" She playfully punches my arm. "When we scrimmage against each other in practice and you come racing down the field with that look in your eyes, I know it'll take everything I've got to try to stop you from scoring." She raises her hand and gives me five. "Be a beast today, Tess!"

⚽

The ref calls the captains and coaches to midfield for the pregame talk and coin toss. "If there is any taunting from the fans or the players, I promise you the red card will be out of my pocket so fast—and the offending player will be out of the game," she warns. Apparently, she heard how physical the last match was.

We shake hands, say "Good luck," and prepare to defend our side of the field since Ramapo won the toss. I remember something Luke once said to me—it's not about luck, it's about skill. I smile at Katie and Brittany. "Good skill," I say.

"Remember our game plan, Tess. You've got to come back on defense when you can, to mark number three," Coach says.

Suddenly, my legs feel rubbery, and I wonder if I have the strength to play both ends of the field. Maybe Coach shouldn't count on me. I'll try my best not to let her down.

Up in the stands, my dad is trying to figure out all the options on his new digital video camera. Mom gave it to him for his birthday three months ago, but we still have more film of feet, sky, and strangers passing by than of anything else.

Ibby waves a homemade sign that says, *Go Lions! Score a goal, Munro!*

Mark's busy talking with Jillian. If I ask him, he won't even be able to tell me the score after the game's over.

The whistle sounds, and suddenly, an army of players in red jerseys surges across midfield line. I take off after #3, who dribbles the ball hard up the middle, looking to her wings to launch a pass. But not before I get my foot in there and disrupt the play. She almost trips and I hear her curse out loud as she fights to regain her balance.

"No way are you walking all over us this time," I say under my breath. It's going to be a battle to the very last whistle.

And it is.

At halftime, the score is tied at 2–2.

I greedily gulp from my water bottle and look into the stands, where I notice three things: Dad's abandoned all hope of working the video, Mom—late as usual—hasn't even arrived yet, and Mark, surprisingly, is totally into the game, shouting brotherly encouragement—"Get the lead out of your butt, Munro!"

I can't get water down my throat quickly enough during the brief ten-minute break. There's an autumn–burning-leaves smell in the air. The sun is just about to set and it's chilly. Even so, I pour the remaining water over my head in order to cool my throbbing red face.

"This is it, girls," Coach says, "our last game, against the only team that's beaten us all year. You've got to play your hearts out these next thirty minutes. And if you do, you'll walk off this field tonight satisfied and proud!"

We each place one hand in the middle and rest the other on the shoulders of our teammates standing next to us. We cheer for the very last time this season, "Go, fight, win— *Lions!*"

Before running out onto the field, Brit does her little kick, where she jumps into the air, clicking her cleats together before she lands, for good luck.

Katie, who's covered with dirt from her aggressive defensive plays in front of our goal, hugs my shoulders and says, "We're going to win, Tess. I just know it!"

Bo's roaring like a wild lion in the stands as he leaps and runs up and down the metal bleachers. He's creating such a racket that the ref eyes him reproachfully. Ibby gives him a good whomp on the head with her cardboard sign to calm him down.

I've got to score another goal, I say to myself as we line up at midfield for the kickoff. The two previous ones mean nothing. It might as well be 0–0 as far as I'm concerned, because I'm not settling for a tie. Not on our last game of the year. Not against this team!

When the whistle blows, Alison taps the ball in front of my feet and, from the corner of my eye, I see #3 charging at me with the intent of getting possession of the ball, no matter what. I've been at the receiving end of her powerful foot and will do my best to avoid coming in contact with it again.

Both teams battle hard at midfield for control of the ball, but neither seems to create the opportunity for scoring that winning goal. With just three minutes remaining in the game, my heart pounds in my chest like it's about to break my ribs. My legs feel like there are twenty-pound sandbags tied to each of them, and I can barely lift my arm for a routine throw-in, and wind up getting called for an illegal throw.

Coach throws her clipboard on the ground. "For cryin' out loud, Tess! Fundamentals! Stay focused. Less than two minutes to play!"

I'm so embarrassed. I can't even meet her eyes. How could I mess up an easy throw-in?

Ramapo is awarded possession and they toss it to #3, who takes off down the field so fast I find myself five yards behind and struggling to catch her.

Thank God for Katie.

She charges out of the penalty area and goes head-to-head with the blond bomber, harassing her for control of the ball.

I race up from behind and slide-tackle her—just getting the tip of my cleat on the ball and sending it wide, but not before a Ramapo striker runs on it, kicking it toward our goal.

I hold my breath and watch the potential game-winning goal sail . . . two feet wide of our net!

I pound my fist on the ground. "Too close!" I cry.

On the scoreboard, there's less than a minute remaining in regulation play, and we have possession—a goal kick. Katie runs on the ball and sends it flying over everyone's heads to midfield, where I'm waiting, hoping, dying for one more chance to take it to the goal and win the game.

Ramapo's defensive line is pushed way up in an attempt to draw us offsides. If I can just beat the center fullback, then I'll have a fast break to the goal. A goal—God! How sweet would that be?

Ms. Poe always says that history repeats itself. And it does out here on the field today.

Having beaten the exhausted fullback, I race with every last bit of strength I have left toward the goal, about twenty yards in front of me. I'm just about to blast a kick into the upper right corner of the net, when I feel a stabbing pain against my shins and my legs suddenly go out from underneath me.

My last vision of the ball before I crash to the ground is it dribbling nonthreateningly right into the goalie's arms.

The whistle shrills. "Foul!" shouts the ref, pulling out a red card and ejecting #3 from the game.

Now, the other team's coach is throwing his clipboard, kicking his bench, and screaming at his player—his best player—#3.

She offers her hand to help me up, hangs her head, and walks away from the scene of the crime.

Number 3 had no choice but to prevent me from scoring any way she could. If it meant taking me down and taking the foul, then so be it. Hey, it's a contact sport. If you don't like it, put on a pair of shorts that say *Dance* and get your butt off the field. It was a calculated foul. After all, I missed the penalty shot in the last game. I might miss again. *If* coach even lets me take it again.

I'm afraid to look at her. I'm torn between hope and dread for what she might signal.

I'm the captain, the highest-scoring forward on this team—in fact, on any team she has ever coached. I should take the penalty kick!

But what if I choke? I missed this very same shot and lost the game, ruined our undefeated season, less than two weeks ago. Why should she trust me to make it this time? Will she give me a second chance?

Katie runs toward me and my teeth clench with disappointment. I guess Coach has signaled her to take the penalty kick and win the game. She has the second-best foot on the team, and I'll just have to accept the decision. But still, I feel hot tears threatening to spill over. I try to blink them back, refusing to cry in front of everyone.

Katie reaches me and puts her arm over my shoulders. "You okay, Tess?"

I hear the concern in her voice and feel guilty. "I'm fine— good skill, Katie. Kick it home."

"I'm not taking the kick," she says.

Confused, I turn and face Coach, who's gesturing for me to take the penalty kick.

I feel all the tension and pain drain from my body. I hold my head up and take a deep breath. She still believes in me!

I place the ball on the white line ten feet in front of the Ramapo goalie, who's swaying back and forth on the balls of her feet like a cat ready to pounce on her prey.

"Not this time," I say under my breath. "This time, it's mine."

The ref blows her whistle.

I don't take my eyes off the ball as I run at it with all my might.

Sometimes—from the very first instant you connect—you just know it's going to be good.

And it is—*goal!*

Driving home from the game, I replay that game-winning penalty kick in my mind over and over again. We defeated our crosstown rivals, the Ramapo Warriors, 3–2, and we celebrated as if we had just won the Olympics or World Cup Soccer.

When we drop Jillian off in front of her house, before closing the car door, she leans in and whispers, "You're a beast, Tess!"

This time, I know it's a compliment.

CHAPTER EIGHTEEN

My history teacher also once said *You can win the battle but lose the war.*

When I woke up this morning and learned that the school levy failed by only forty-nine votes, I understood what that expression means. If I had the choice between winning our soccer game yesterday or winning the vote, I would have chosen for the long term, for the greater good—and given up that most beautiful win against Ramapo.

"You can't always pick and choose your victories, Tess. Sometimes you have to accept the defeats and move on," my mother says over her morning coffee and paper.

I won't accept.

I can't stop crying.

I refuse to move on.

I wish there were some leftover Halloween pumpkins from Ibby's party. I'd love to smash a few—hundred. And what's there to move on to, if there're no sports at school anymore? Battle ball's just not going to cut it.

⚽

At school, it feels like a funeral. The principals, teachers, and most of the students walk around with their heads hanging low. We use our library voices even in the hallways. Bo's

I write back:

Ibby,
The jeans suck. The levy sucks. Life sucks! Now I'll
have to get a ride to school with Mark!? Harper cried 2nd
period. Couldn't look at her because then I'd start
crying again, too.
        Tess
P.S. Got any leftover pumpkins at your house?

I fold the note into the shape of a paper airplane and wait
until Mr. Chen writes on the board before recklessly sending it
Ibby's way.

Never fly a plane when you're depressed.

It crashes into the back of Olivia's hair, and she turns
around, glaring at me.

I give her a look that says if she doesn't pass this note to
Ibby immediately, there will be hell to pay, and this time, she'll
be lucky if her shoes are the only thing I kick.

Olivia pulls the paper plane out of her hair, checks Chen's
location in front of the board, and passes the note to Ibs.

"Thanks," I whisper.

"You're welcome."

I guess she's feeling the loss, too. No more cheerleading.
No more putting her half-naked body on display every Friday
for Spirit Day and football and basketball games, too.

"That doesn't make sense!" insists Bo. "Why would Atticus
take the Tom Robinson case if he knew he was going to lose
anyway?"

dressed in black and wears a black armband. "I'm in mourning," he explains. "They've killed sports!"

Ms. Harper actually bursts into tears during the middle of class. Joey Montanado asks her if she's crying because the levy failed or because she might lose her job.

"Both," she sobs.

In English, Mr. Chen tries to wrap up *To Kill a Mockingbird*, but most of us, especially the athletes and kids that know their after-school clubs will be cut, find it hard to concentrate on Maycomb County's problems. We have enough of our own to think about.

When Mr. Chen's back is turned, Ibby quickly tosses me a note. It lands right in front of my nose, since my head is resting on my arm on the desk. I check to see if Mr. Chen is looking and then I open it. No pretty gel-penned flowers this time.

Tess,

Soooo sorry. Dad says they'll vote again in the spring. You'll play sports! Awesome game yesterday! You're amazing!!!

Luv you, Ibs

P.S. Your jeans were great!

Mr. Chen is talking about the major themes in the novel and preparing us for a one-paragraph expository essay that we'll have to write. I could care less about the essay. I've decided to run away and join a European soccer team where they have their priorities straight. They don't have stupid school levies, and people start riots for their favorite soccer teams.

"Is there something to be learned from losing?" asks Mr. Chen.

"No!" I shout.

The entire class stares at the crazy girl with the puffy red eyes and the pathetic jeans.

"There's *nothing* to be learned from losing," I say. "Losing sucks . . . and—" I feel the tears well up in my eyes. Everyone's face looks blurry. "And it's senseless and . . ." I put my head back down on the desk. "I haven't learned a thing," I whisper.

Mr. Chen ignores "sucks" and nods sympathetically. "I'm sorry, Tess. I know how disappointed you and many people are feeling today that the school levy failed. But I have confidence that if you want to play sports, you have the patience and the persistence to figure something out."

⚽

Mr. Chen is right. I'll figure out a way to play. That afternoon, I called a few soccer players I know from my summer league who play for Suffern City Schools and asked them how they continued their sports programs after their levy failed.

So, I have to head up a few fund-raisers and help raise the money for a Pay to Play program in our district. Hey, it's better than listening to Olivia Fletcher boss me around until the next levy, this spring.

We've raised three hundred dollars so far. If I can raise four hundred and fifty more by November 15, there will be a Clarkstown Lions Middle School Girls' Basketball team this winter.

I picture myself on the foul line in our new basketball

uniforms—okay, ditch the new uniforms; we're on a budget. Tie score. Two seconds left in double overtime. If I make the basket, we win the middle school championship. I take a few practice bounces to loosen up. Deep breath. Think BEEF. Balance. Eyes on basket. Elbows in. Follow through—*swish!* Tess Munro scores the winning basket! The crowd goes wild as the buzzer sounds!

The door opens.

Jillian O'Hanlon pops her head outside and asks, "What are you doing out here, Tess? It's snowing out!"

I wave colorful fund-raising brochures in front of her face. *Oops*—made her flinch. "Want to buy some magazines?" I ask.

"What do you have?"

"Um . . . I've got *National Geographic, Popular Mechanics, Good Housekeeping*—"

"Ah . . . Tess."

"*Sports Illustrated, Time, Scientific American*—"

"Tess!"

"Huh?"

"*Glamour* or *Cosmo*."

"Oh." I frantically scan my list. "Got 'em both!"

She holds the door wide open. "Come on in."

Jillian's home smells like pumpkin pie, nail polish, Pop Tarts, and poodles. As she hangs up my scarf and coat, I think of Soccer Chick Rule Number 7 – Never, ever give up!

Oh, and one more thing—Soccer chicks *rule!!!*

12 06